YOU HAVE INCREDIBLE PSYCHIC ABILITIES . . .

You just need to know how to use them! This remarkable guide lets you try your hand at a number of different divinatory practices. It provides tips on harnessing your hidden powers of prediction . . . shows you how to prepare both the mind and spirit to receive and interpret the information you need . . . and helps you open your mind to the powers you never thought you had:

- **Crystal gazing to release your psychic energy centers**

- **Automatic writing to get in touch with your spirit guides**

- **Using the pendulum to predict the sex of an unborn child**

- **And much more . . .**

THE DIVINATION HANDBOOK

Crawford Q. Kennedy

An Armadillo Press Book

A SIGNET BOOK

NEW AMERICAN LIBRARY

A DIVISION OF PENGUIN BOOKS USA INC.

This book is for entertainment purposes only. The author makes no claims as to the accuracy of the information derived from the use of the methods and materials listed in this book, nor is it guaranteed that such methods, traditions, and folklore contained herein will provide the seeker the means to adequately determine what has not yet come to pass.

Copyright © 1989 by Armadillo Press

SIGNET TRADEMARK REG. U.S. PAT. OFF. AND FOREIGN COUNTRIES
REGISTERED TRADEMARK—MARCA REGISTRADA
HECHO EN DRESDEN, TN, U.S.A.

SIGNET, SIGNET CLASSIC, MENTOR, ONYX, PLUME, MERIDIAN and NAL BOOKS are published by New American Library, a division of Penguin Books USA Inc., 1633 Broadway, New York, New York 10019

First Printing, January, 1990

1 2 3 4 5 6 7 8 9

PRINTED IN THE UNITED STATES OF AMERICA

To Edward Claflin

Special thanks to Jack Andrew Earley
for the *puttanesca*.

Contents

Introduction

Divination, fortune-telling—the words themselves conjure up pictures of wizened crones, bizarre predictions, and inescapable, unalterable Fate. The practice of divination dates back thousands of years, and some of the most highly respected methods of divination can be seen in the light of modern times as, well, downright pedestrian: no more mysterious than a bowl of water, a needle and thread, or a deck of playing cards.

If divination practices, as wide and varied as they can be, may be given a general definition, it is simply this: Divination is the ability, through any one of a number of methods, to tap into a subconscious awareness of events—past, present, or future—usually through the use of symbols.

If the methods of divination collected here seem strange or alien to the reader, it is because most of those methods are intentionally designed to allow the diviner to put aside his rational, logical, conscious mind and tap into the larger, more spiritual, and—many believe collective—unconscious. It is that area of the mind where, if you will, "everything is known" and, therefore, knowable.

There is almost no one alive who does not have questions—about the future, about the present, about others. Our questions about our lives are as varied as our individual personalities, and there are very few of us who are willing to wait for the answers to those questions to unfold with time, especially if we may have the ability to tap into information that may change our futures for the better. And yet, because we are individuals, not every personality is able to readily respond to or interpret every set of available symbols when it comes to getting answers to those questions or getting the information we feel we must have. Just as some people find it easier to learn French than they do German, some people will find the symbolic language of the Tarot, for example, much easier to understand and interpret than working with a pendulum or Ouija board. There are some who receive a great amount of telepathic information through dreams and only need help in reading the symbols contained in their dreams to better divine their message. Others are more comfortable with physical evidence, better able to read actual shapes and symbols divined in methods such as tealeaf- or wax-reading.

The point is, this book is designed for experiment. It is to be used as an introduction, not a comprehensive guide, to the many different methods of divination; using the basic methods contained in these pages, readers are encouraged to try their hand at a number of different divinatory practices until they find the one that will prove right and most reliable for them. Do not be discouraged if your initial attempts result in confusing or contradictory answers. Psychic and divinatory skills are very much like the muscles of the physical body: They must be exercised and developed before they can be relied upon to behave with maximum efficiency.

THE
DIVINATION
HANDBOOK

How to Use This Book

All human beings have psychic intuition. Your intuitive powers can be developed at any time or any stage in your life. With practice, a playful attitude, and honest awareness, anyone can get results from the methods of divination outlined in this book. This chapter gives tips and practical information that many psychics and awareness specialists have used throughout the ages to prepare both mind and spirit to openly receive and accurately interpret the information that is all around you.

Using and Trusting Your Instincts

The best place to begin is always at the beginning. Before you actually sit down to read the entries in this book, find yourself a place and time where you are comfortable, relaxed, and unlikely to be disturbed. Begin your search for a practical method of divination by simply thumbing through this book, taking note of those entries and methods that you find particularly attractive. Chances are, your inner mind is already guiding you to the methods that are best suited to your needs and personality.

Mental Preparation

In all divinatory literature, myths and stories abound about just what constitutes the proper mental preparation before undertaking a reading. Some seers and psychics find it necessary to fall into a trance. Edgar Cayce, the well-known prophet and clairvoyant, was a strait-laced Baptist minister whose conscious beliefs were so deeply ingrained that he could only give a reading while he was asleep! Too, there are examples of people who had to go into seclusion, undertake fasts, and what have you before they considered themselves cleansed enough of wordly distraction to glean any accurate information from their psychic selves.

Yet for the most part, heavy or prolonged preparation prior to undertaking a reading is unnecessary, particularly for a novice. The following simple suggestions are sure to help and will begin to foster the state of mind you need to achieve results, no matter what form of divination you decide is best for you.

Step One: Free yourself from distraction. It is important to find a quiet time of the day during which you will not be disturbed as you present your queries. Candles, soft music, or environmental tapes may relax you. Foster an unstrained concentration and allow your mind to go free. What we are after is a relaxed "disassociation of consciousness." To describe this is easy; to achieve it is something else. It is best not to start out by trying to "make your mind a blank," because the mind is never blank. Chances are, shutting yourself away in a dark room and blanking out is only going to result in your worrying about the grocery list or the accuracy of your latest bank statement. For this reason, it helps to find a point of concentration. By focusing your attention on a crystal ball or a candle flame, for example, you are essentially achieving what might be called a state of visual boredom, inhibiting the activity of the cerebral cortex. By concentrating on one signal, the candle flame, you are filtering out other external sensory input. This frees the mind, in effect, to wander within.

Step Two: It is essential to remain open and playful. This does not mean that you should not take the divinatory arts seriously but only that you should not undertake them with an excess of rigid expectations. If you ask a certain question and get an answer to a completely different issue, be open to the fact that perhaps you have asked an incomplete question. Novices should never begin by asking their most serious or important questions. Instead, try warming up to a particular method by asking two or three questions of lesser consequence.

Step Three: Gather information without judgment. When getting a reading, absorb all the information that you can, whether or not it would seem to apply to the question at hand; you can sort out the logistics later. There are two parts to every reading; the intuitive knowledge that comes to you in your altered state, and the rational interpretation you apply to the question at hand. Remember to consider all the information you receive and try to avoid making editorial judgments. This is especially important when reading for others. Do not use this situation as an opportunity to tell others how to live their lives. You are not necessarily responsible for applying your psychic findings to your friends', neighbors', or relatives' problems. That's their job, not yours.

Step Four: Avoid too much emotional involvement with the question. If you are worried or excessively wishful about the outcome of a reading, you will find ways to engineer the information into the answers you want rather than discovering the answers that are being given to you. Again, this is easier said than done and may not always be easily achieved. Yet it is important to try to disassociate yourself from the emotional implications of a question before attempting to answer it as much as you are able. Do not query when you are upset, anxious, stressed, or otherwise lacking objectivity. Frantic questioning and cross-examination of any method of divination will only result in confusion and chaos, some of which can be downright misleading and all of which must be sorted through at a later date to better discern the clear answer you are being supplied.

Step Five: Avoid attempting a reading when you are fatigued. Readings should be done in a relaxed state. This is quite different from a state of exhaustion. Make sure you are well rested before doing your reading. This will help you to be alert to the nuances of the information received as well as keeping you from rushing through it in an effort to get your answers as quickly as possible. Readings take time and concentration, neither of which are peak considerations when you are tired.

Spiritual Preparation

Purifying your motives: It is important that you begin with unselfish motives. Determine, first of all, that the information you receive will be used to help others and yourself to fulfill your true potential, not to engineer results that will hamper or hurt those around you. Remember that information is only information. It can be used in many ways. If you use your psychic findings to further yourself at the cost of others or the world with which you interact, you might find the information you receive becoming unclear, twisted, and confusing. True psychic insight is never confusing. It is clear and unmuddied by personal considerations and often liberating in its implications. If you find yourself receiving confusing information, take a minute to recheck your motives and intentions.

Psychic protection: There will undoubtedly come a time in your psychic growth when you will need some psychic protection. For this reason, it is important to get into the habit of psychic protection from the very start. At the beginning of any reading, even before you open your mind, surround yourself with white light. Whether you mentally identify this light as the light of God, the light of the sun, or simply positive energy, the implications are the same—purity, strength, and protection. There are many methods for creating the cone of white light, but the important thing to remember is to start at the crown of your head and cover your body with light until you reach the soles of your feet. Imagine yourself pulsing with the energy of that light, radiating it all around you. It may help you to spend a few moments each day upon waking up by surrounding yourself with a cone of light. You may then augment this just before you decide to do your reading.

Be sensitive to your instruments. Whatever the method of divination, the instruments can be subject to negative influences, and it is important to maintain a sensitivity, a "feel," for them and to understand what that feeling is telling you. Perhaps you are using a crystal ball or a set of Tarot cards soaked with questionable energy. Your readings are becoming strange, peculiar, or odd. Don't panic. There are many things you can do to remedy the situation and get yourself back on track.

If negative energy is clinging to a physical object, you can bury it in salt overnight or burn dried sage so the smoke covers the object. If the energy is clinging to your self, you can take salt baths (mix a handful of table salt in your bathwater after tossing the water thoroughly with a bucket or saucepan). As you end your bath, take a moment to concentrate on the sticky, dark energy leaving your body and going down the drain.

Another effective method of protection is to visualize yourself in a beautiful garden. It can be any kind of garden you like—it's yours. Picture a warm, sunlit day with wispy clouds in a bright blue sky. When you have your garden constructed exactly the way you want it, build walls around it. The walls will protect you.

Following are other hints that will help you open your mind as well as protect you psychically:

Create a psychic workroom: During a time in which you are sure you won't be disturbed lie down in a comfortable place, close your eyes, and imagine yourself in beautiful natural surroundings, the sun shining down on you and filling you with its warmth. Once you feel relaxed and self-assured, take in your surroundings and choose a location for your psychic workroom. Mentally build a center and fill it with your favorite furnishings. Be conscious of the details of this place; paint it your favorite color and imagine yourself vibrating in harmony with that color. Give yourself tools with which to operate—perhaps a large book in which all the information in the world is written down, both past and future. If you like, you can provide a telephone by which you can contact anyone in the world or by which anyone can contact you. Build a large movie screen on which can be shown anything you like and on which visual images can be slowed down, replayed, or fast-forwarded. Maybe you would like to include a calendar of all past and future events you will ever want to know. You can come to this room at any time and access the information provided here.

Crystal meditation: Some people find crystal work helpful in opening up psychic-energy centers. Quartz has been shown to be effective for this purpose. Take a piece of quartz, surround it with white light, and place it on your forehead. Visualize a stream of white or golden light flowing through the crystal into the point on your forehead centered between your eyebrows, clearing away all psychic debris and bringing with it a sense of well-being.

Reading for others: To tune yourself into the energy of other people, take a moment to touch their hand and allow yourself to tune into how they feel and the sort of energy in which they are operating. This will enable you to impart the information you have gotten for them in ways they will better understand. If, upon touching another person, you feel uncomfortable and wish to release the energy immediately, touch the wall, the floor, or a table and imagine the energy flowing out of your fingertips into the surface you have chosen for energy release.

Hint: Remember that psychic information is not fact. Free will is as important in shaping the future as any information you retrieve from your reading. Use the things you discover to help in making decisions and give you more data to use in solving problems or anticipating the possible results of certain methods of action. Always remember that the future is not written in stone. Just because you see something with clarity does not mean it cannot be changed. Any person who relies solely on psychic information to determine his or her future is like someone driving down the road and reading a roadmap without ever looking out of the window. Psychic information is meant to augment experience, not substitute for the obvious.

Biblical Divination

Essentially, biblical divination involves the use of the Bible as an oracle. Despite the fact that biblical divination is often thought to be as old as the Bible itself, the use of books as oracles predates the Christian era by thousands of years. In the Orient, we can find the antecedent of biblical divination in the use of the still-popular I Ching, while in the West Virgil's *Aeneid* was popularly used as an oracle in the Middle Ages, after the fall of the Roman Empire. In fact, predictions gained from poetic passages of *The Aeneid* were thought to be so accurate that Virgil gained a surprising posthumous reputation as a magician rather than a poet! People made regular pilgrimages to his grave at Naples, where miracles were reported to take place, and magicians traveled there from all over Europe to pay him homage.

It wasn't until the Protestant Reformation, as the Bible itself first became widely available, that biblical divination came into its own. It was then that the Good Book came to be looked upon by Europeans as the wisest, most accurate, and most sincere of all oracle books. As a matter of fact, John Wesley, founder of the Methodist Church, was reported by many sources to open the Bible and pick out a passage at random when members of his brethren came to him seeking spiritual guidance and answers to their problems.

While it is highly unlikely that Wesley referred to his method of gleaning guidance from the Bible as divination, or to the Bible itself as an oracle, the methods he used to find his answers are in the best traditions of oracle-book fortune-telling.

Simply put, the method is as follows:

The querent has only to meditate upon his problem or question, and with that fixed firmly in his thoughts, he then opens the Bible three times at random, each time letting his finger fall by chance on a particular verse or passage. Each of the three passages is then interpreted—either literally or metaphorically—and applied to the case at hand.

From a purely divinatory standpoint, the problem with the Bible—and, in fact, any oracle book used in this manner—is that the answers given can be quite obscure and demand much in the way of interpretation. Biblical divination is best employed, then, by people whose background and/or religious affiliations have equipped them to best understand the Good Book and its inherent spiritual messages or by those who feel a special affinity with the Word. This does not mean that you must necessarily be a theologian to use the Bible for divinatory means, only that a general understanding of it prior to employing it as an oracle book will better prepare you to apply the answers put forth by this method to your specific questions and situations.

Candles, Divination by (Lychnoscopy)

The use of candles has been recommended for centuries in all sorts of magical and divinatory rites and ceremonies, and even now, regardless of unlimited access to electricity, it is hard to conjure up an image of a seance, fortune-teller, or crystal diviner without also including the ubiquitous presence of candles and their unique, mysterious light—the special atmosphere only candlelight can provide.

Perhaps it is because of the special, almost psychic atmosphere created by candlelight that diviners first began to infuse the candle with predictive powers of its own. Divination by candles, or *lychnoscopy*, is a type of divination by fire that involves the focusing of one's concentration on one or more candle flames, reading, and then interpreting the subtleties of the burning wick according to the question asked. While there are infinite variations recommended throughout occult literature as to the sizes, colors, and types of candles used in readings of this kind, the interpretations for the actions of the flame and wick seem to remain curiously the same, regardless of the type of candle used.

Included below are two basic beginner's methods for a lychnoscopic reading, along with some traditional interpretations. Remember, though, that no mere list of interpretations, however time honored, can give you the most accurate picture of coming events. Candle-reading first involves candle-gazing and the focus of your concentration upon the flame. That alone may be enough to open you up psychically, so if you are aware of any additional impressions during your candle-reading, be sure to use them to augment the interpretations provided here.

Method 1: To find out a simple answer to a yes or no question, light a new candle in a color that corresponds to your astrological sign or, if the querent is someone else, their sign. Use red or orange candles for the fire signs—Aries, Leo, and Sagittarius; blue candles for the water signs—Cancer, Scorpio, and Pisces; green for the earth signs—Taurus, Virgo, and Capricorn; and white for the air signs—Gemini, Libra, and Aquarius.

While meditating on the question, light the candle in a draft-free room. Continue concentrating while the candle burns. If the flame leans in the direction of the querent and the wick curves likewise, the answer to the question is yes. If the wick and flame burn away from you, the answer is likely to be no. A variation on this method involves love and romance: To discover if a lover is sincere, light a candle that corresponds to his or her astrological sign and, while concentrating on a picture or mental image of the person, ask if they truly love you. Again, if the wick burns in your direction, the answer is yes. If the wick burns away from you, the lover is not sincere and you are likely to be better off looking elsewhere.

Method 2: This method is best used with less specific questions. Arrange three candles of fine wax in a triangle, each candle equidistant from the others. In a draft-free room, light the candles in a clockwise direction. Study the flames carefully. If a flame moves in a steady pattern from left to right, it means a change of residence or relocation coming up. If a flame or flames rotate in a roughly circular formation, it foretells that the querent is at risk from enemies and had best watch his or her back in the near future. Should one candle burn brighter than the other two, it signals unexpected windfalls or good fortune. Should one or more of the flames throw out sparks, it is considered a warning: be careful and cautious, for you may have disappointments ahead. If one flame burns much brighter than the other two, it signals increasing success over a period of time and possibly a person who will achieve fame and greatness in their lifetime. Yet if a flame flares for just a moment, that greatness is likely to be fleeting. And, as you might expect, if a flame sputters or dies out, it is a tragic portent—death or catastrophe, for the querent or someone close to them, is likely to be near.

Cards, Playing

While the origins of the four suits of contemporary playing cards can undoubtedly
be traced back to the Minor Arcana of the
far older Tarot deck, the ordinary deck has,
over the years, acquired divinatory significance and a tradition in fortune-telling quite
apart from that of its honored ancestor.

In fact, many diviners prefer playing cards
as a tool for answering the questions of daily
life, solving personal problems, and foresee-
ing the future, simply because the readings
put forth by ordinary cards dictate more
practical, easy-to-understand answers—often
quite removed from the more mystical (and
sometimes cryptic!) language of the Tarot.
Other fortune-tellers believe playing cards to
have numerological significance: appear-
ances of a 4 of any suit in a spread, for instance, would foretell trials of some sort, 4
being the number of Saturn, the planet of
discipline. Still others have used playing

cards to pinpoint coming events by their correspondence to the calendar. They believe the fifty-two cards in an ordinary playing deck correspond to the fifty-two weeks in a year. The cards are divided into four suits, each corresponding to a season of the year—diamonds for spring, hearts for summer, clubs for autumn, and spades for winter. Each suit is comprised of thirteen cards, supposed to roughly correspond to the thirteen weeks of each season.

Yet despite how much or how little significance you may attach to the above theories, or how much you may know of the Tarot, you will find that the playing deck does have much in common with its older cousin when it comes to the general divinatory meanings of the cards themselves. You may also find that once you have mastered the methods of divining with playing cards, they can serve as a practical and useful prelude should you wish to "graduate" to the more difficult and involved systems of the Tarot itself.

The Suits

The suit of hearts is believed to have been derived from the corresponding suit of cups in the Tarot's Minor Arcana. As one might expect, this suit is believed to rule the emotions, social relationships, and affairs of the heart. A preponderance of hearts in a spread will undoubtedly speak to the emotional life of the querent, regardless of the question at hand.

Diamonds is the suit of luck and adventure, exciting news, or turns of events. Like the corresponding Tarot suit of wands, many diamonds in a spread is sure to signal excitement, activity, and coming changes (though, of course, the exact cards will determine the specifics).

Spades is the suit of upheaval. There are more cards of misfortune in this suit than in any other. Many spades in a spread does not, however, necessarily mean outright disaster. More likely, it means that the querent is due for a shake-up or two, or that he or she will have to earn what they want from life. The suit of spades corresponds to the Tarot suit of swords.

Related to the Tarot suit of coins or pentacles, the suit of clubs rules the material world, and questions regarding money, worldly goods, or financial problems are almost sure to have some clubs showing up in the spread. Here too is where to look when concerned with questions of legacies, inheritance, and material gains or losses.

The Face Cards

Generally, face cards showing up in a playing-card spread will correspond to personalities, male and female, displaying the nature of the suit. A Queen of hearts, for example, indicates the presence of a tender-hearted, emotional woman in the querent's life, while a Queen of clubs will denote a woman who is secure, comfortably well off, and perhaps tight with her purse-strings, and so on. Jacks can denote either a young male or female but are generally thought to be feminine when they are in the "feminine" suits (hearts and clubs), while the Jacks of diamonds and spades (the "masculine" suits) generally denote the presence of a young man. Refer to the list of specific meanings that follows for further details.

How to Read Playing Cards: Some Sample Methods

The Wish Spread

This is by far the easiest method of all to use and to interpret, since only two of the fifty-two cards in a playing deck are given any divinatory significance at all—the 9 of hearts and the 10 of spades. In this spread, the questioner asks only, "Will I get my wish?" and concentrates on his or her wish as things proceed. Shuffle the cards three times, cut the deck (or, if you are reading for someone else, have them cut it) and begin to lay the cards out in rows of thirteen. If the 9 of hearts (the Wish Card) is turned up first, the questioner will get his wish. On the other hand, if the 10 of spades (the Disappointment Card) is turned up first, the querent will not get his wish.

The Nine-Card Spread

Slightly more difficult, yet certainly less limited, is the nine-card spread, sometimes called the Past, Present, and Future spread. It is best suited to general readings regarding the querent and nonspecific inquiries—for instance, his or her general circumstances, the love life, or questions regarding his or her financial condition. Thus, if someone asks you, "Will I ever find a boyfriend?" or "When am I going to make some money?" this would be the spread to use.

The cards are shuffled and cut three times in the direction of the querent. They are then dealt, face up, in three rows of three cards each. The top row represents the past, the center row, the present, and the third row the future. In the past and future rows, the cards are read from left to right, by position, thus:

The Distant Past	Past Two or Three Years	Immediate Past
Present		
Immediate Future	Short-term Future	Long-term Future

By far the *most important* thing to recall in doing this or any other kind of card-reading is to *first read the cards in relation to each other* before attempting to interpret each card's specific meaning. For example, if the querent is asking about an improvement in finances and he or she turns up the 7 of hearts in the immediate-future position, followed by a 5 of clubs and 9 of diamonds, it could be considered confusing, since, read individually the cards indicate (a) the "triumph of Venus," (b) quarrels and disappointments in business, and (c) birth, marriage, or prosperity. Yet when read in relation to one another, this group of cards clearly indicates that the querent's improvement in finances is going to come out of an emotional association with another person. That relationship, however, will lead to some serious disagreements over money, yet the 9 of diamonds indicates that despite some upheaval there will be a change for the better and the disagreements will prove productive in the long term.

The Meanings of the Cards

Remember that no mere list of interpretations is going to adequately constitute the "meanings" of a deck of cards, as all such lists are necessarily arbitrary, as they cannot encompass the interrelationships of cards in a particular spread or how a particular card relates to a question. That is where the reader comes in. Your intuition and intelligence is more than half of what constitutes any card-reading, and you should never hesitate to bring those things into play when studying a list. Consider the following interpretations as you might ingredients in a recipe: Eggs, milk, and flour can make popovers or pancakes; how the ingredients are combined is what determines the result.

Hearts

Ace: Literally, this is the card of happiness; by itself, it indicates great joy, and the cards around it will indicate those things or people that make the querent happiest.

2: Friendship or partnership, emotionally rather than materially based.

3: Sociability, celebration, and, in some instances, sexual encounters.

4: Marriage, love, and solid emotional attachments.

5: Unsure love, or love that turns to hatred or disappointment; emotional uncertainty.

6: Benevolence, established affection; a pleasant invitation.

7: The "triumph of Venus": love fulfilled; sexual passion.

8: Intellectual love or love tempered by reason; also communications of love.

9: The Wish Card: The querent will get his wish when the 9 is surrounded by favorable cards. Depending on the preponderant suit surrounding this card, the wish will come true in areas of love, money, et cetera. When surrounded by negative cards, this card can mean excess or overindulgence; remember the adage "be careful what you wish for—you might get it."

10: Love untroubled by financial concerns; comfort, prosperity, and fertility.

Jack: An impulsive lover; love at first sight; great affection.

Queen: A tender-hearted, emotional woman; receptivity to love.

King: A man, young or old, desirous of love.

Spades

Ace: A new adventure, an opportunity; the cards around it will likely indicate whether the outcome will prove satisfying.

2: A hopeful beginning; general forward movement of affairs; also tension between opposing forces.

3: Careful consideration of future plans; meetings, conferences.

4: Luck that results from careful planning and foresight.

5: Violent disagreements, quarrels, and disputes; plans going wrong; unforeseen circumstances and conflicts.

6: Slow progress to the point of frustration; steady movement but without gratification.

7: The end of a romance; accidents and misunderstandings.

8: Be prepared for the unexpected; communications, journeys, and unexpected arrivals or departures.

9: Family arguments, usually between parents and children; the elderly becoming a burden; daily annoyances.

10: The Disappointment Card: The querent will not get his wish. Should the surrounding cards be fortunate, it means that the good fortune indicated will be somehow diminished or flawed; if unfortunate cards surround, the querent is in for hard times.

Jack: A young person, usually a young man, who is full of ideas and inspirations, but often short on follow-through; seduction through the cerebral.

Queen: A quick-witted woman, often sharp-tongued but very charming; can mean mourning or infertility.

King: A man who is vital and exciting; a risk-taker, with many ideas, thoughts, and designs; an adventurer.

Diamonds

Ace: Good but erratic luck; surprises; an energetic beginning.

2: Increase in prosperity but at a price; a caution to be prudent or relax.

3: Luck through teamwork and cooperation; progress.

4: Matters are proceeding splendidly; established success, good fortune; beware of complacency.

5: Conflicts or troubles that result from a difference of opinion or ideals; keep your temper at all costs.

6: A very fortunate card, one that surpasses mere satisfaction; deep happiness; a charmed life.

7: A passionate relationship; a sexual affair; physical comfort of every kind.

8: Messages from afar; holidays and vacations; short-term travel or exciting news.

9: A birth or marriage; an exciting relationship; change for the better or productive disagreements.

10: Happy endings; reward, luxuries; a well-earned rest.

Jack: An agressive young man; impulsive, courageous, and, in some cases, a heartbreaker.

Queen: An energetic woman, possessed of considerable insight; sometimes pushy but well intentioned.

King: A highly competitive man, a workaholic; someone who finds it difficult to relax.

Clubs

Ace: Wealth and prosperity; the beginning of a series of fortunate events.

2: A division of assets; quarrels over money; some material loss but something left over.

3: Inertia; sluggishness in the movement of personal affairs; sometimes indecision.

4: An unexpected stroke of good fortune and financial success.

5: Disputes over money or inheritances; money just out of reach; unexpected obstacles.

6: The querent is "on a roll"; expect a series of fortunate events.

7: Money wasted or frittered away; foolish speculation.

8: Money gained as a result of careful and patient planning; sometimes a warning against the possibility of theft.

9: Joint financial matters, especially regarding spouses, children, or lovers.

10: A stable and prosperous situation; comfort and reward for work well done.

Jack: A young woman involved in financial matters who is not always trustworthy; sometimes indolence or "sour grapes."

Queen: An earth mother, one who is fair but generous with her gifts; stability.

King: A prosperous, secure, and very reliable man; often indicative of the querent's employer.

Coffee Grounds

While almost everyone knows that readings may be obtained from swirling tea leaves in the bottom of a cup, there are few who are aware that the same methodology applies to readings done with coffee grounds. Just as the practice of tealeaf-reading grew up in tea-drinking countries, the practice of reading fortunes in grounds can be traced first to the Turks, then to South America, and finally the United States.

The coffee for this type of reading can be of any variety but is best prepared in a percolator or samovar or by a method that does not require a filter. Clean white porcelain or stoneware cups are best to use as the shapes can be more easily read. The person who requires the reading drinks the coffee, leaving a small amount, one or two sips at most, in the bottom of the cup, Swirl the contents of the cup slowly while concentrating on the question or questions. Allow the liquid to settle and study the formations of the grounds that cling to the sides of the cup. In order to do this, you will need, in effect, to squint and "soften" your vision, allowing your imagination and intuition to roam freely. If you see a shape that resembles more than one thing, combine the readings for greater significance and application.

Symbols that appear near the rim of the cup signify events that will happen within a period of weeks, near the middle of the cup speak for the future six months, and near the bottom of the cup will take a year or more to come to pass.

Below is a list of symbols that may appear in a coffee-ground-reading. It is by no means all inclusive, however, and you must remember to take into account your own personal symbology in order to employ this type of method effectively.

Airplane: An indication of "rising" in the world, rather than of travel; increased prosperity or an inheritance.

Anchor: Indicates happy endings or travels for the good of all.

Arch: Literally, a bridge between two individuals; a meeting with someone who will prove important to your future.

Bell: Good news.

Birds: A good omen for pleasant coming events and news. Clearly, if vultures, buzzards, or other scavengers are indicated, the implications here are altered.

Books: Seek professional advice, greater learning; or more information is needed regarding the matter at hand.

Bottle: Sociability, invitations.

Butterfly: Someone who goes from flower to flower; not a serious relationship.

Chain: Hard work is indicated.

Clock: A significant meeting is coming up.

Cross: Unpleasant news, depending on the symbols nearest it.

Crown: A promotion; desires are attained.

Dart: A happy love affair.

Dice: A warning against speculations and gambling.

Fish: Splendid news from a distant place.

Flag: A very fortunate omen; good fortune of all kinds.

Foot: Stagnation of some kind; resolution of a matter is delayed.

Gate: A sudden change of fortune.

Hammer: More effort is required; apply yourself.

Harp: Worldly prosperity; emotional fulfillment.

Hat: Mishaps; minor misfortunes without lasting effect.

Heart: Excitement in one's emotional life.

Hills or mountains: Problems that must be overcome.

Key: A mystery will be explained.

Knife: Quarrels and conflicts.

Ladder: Things will improve shortly.

Ring: Good luck in one's love life.

Road: If straight, things go well; if crooked, the opposite.

Rocks: Small problems.

Roof: A move or change of location is coming.

Scales: A caution to balance the emotions.

Ship: Good luck from a journey.

Tools: Be careful with money.

Trees: Everything will flourish; a very fortunate sign.

Crystal-Gazing

Crystal-gazing is part of a larger group of divinatory practices called scrying—that is, entering an inner space by gazing fixedly at a clear or translucent surface or object. Crystal-gazing has often been the most derided of the divinatory arts; skeptics and jokesters have found the image of a person staring fixedly at a crystal ball or like object inherently comic in its connotations. Consider the very popular nineteenth-century cartoon that portrays a poster of a woman, complete with a kerchief, her eyes wide and faraway, that advertises "Salon for Crystal Gazing and Palmistry," printed over with the caption "Closed due to unforeseen circumstances."

Yet crystal-gazing and scrying are among the most ancient of all the divinatory arts, and it is not unlikely that a Cro-Magnon or two found themselves occasionaly transfixed by the strange images that appeared as they paused to stare into a pool of water or a running stream.

Perhaps the most psychically dependent and, therefore, subjective of all divinatory methods, crystal-gazing has little in the way of traditional "cookbook" meanings to guide you in the interpretation of your visions. Contrary to popular opinion, most crystal-scryers rarely have detailed visions of the future or see pictures of recognizable individuals moving across the ball like a filmed documentary of what is to come, unless they happen to be extraordinarily visually oriented in the first place.

Needless to say, investment in a true crystal ball, or even one of the more popular shaped and polished glass balls, can prove more investment than the average person is prepared to make. It is best, then, to try your hand at scrying with something simpler, and one of the following suggestions should prove an acceptable substitute: a clear glass or bowl of water (glass with an iridescent finish can be particularly helpful); a dish of black ink or water colored with food coloring; a pool, lake, or even a filled bathtub.

Dim the lights and choose a room and time where you are unlikely to be disturbed. Relax and clear your mind. Unfocus your eyes until you sense your vision start to soften and blur, while keeping your attention fixed on the crystal or whatever substitute you have chosen. Allow your mind to rest; don't attempt to force yourself to see something. If you can keep your attention fixed for more than twenty seconds without any awareness of outside influences—the clock ticking, traffic noise, the sound of your own breathing—you have an exceptional capacity for being able to develop your scrying ability. But whether you are good or bad at first, you can train your mind with repeated attempts, until you find you are able to concentrate for longer and longer periods of time without allowing your mind to be distracted by outside influences.

Those with a natural inclination for this practice will soon begin to see images float to the surface; yet, as mentioned above, it is a mistake to believe that these images will be detailed. More likely these images will appear as clouds, fog, or mist, often tinged with color, and there are many successful scryers who have learned to correctly interpret these clouds and colors according to the descriptions below. Again, do not hesitate to augment these rather inadequate general descriptions with your own psychic or clairvoyant input and impressions.

Blue clouds: These pertain to success in career or business.

Golden clouds: Good finances, prosperity, and a coming or renewed romance.

Gray to black clouds: Ill fortune; the darker the clouds, the worse the portents.

Green clouds: Green is the color of healing and reward; it signifies these things as well as emotional happiness to come.

Orange clouds: Emotional difficulties; hidden anger.

Red clouds: Great danger and the possibility of destruction. Be careful.

Silver clouds: Difficulty followed by good fortune—the silver lining effect.

White clouds: A great good fortune will soon appear.

Yellow clouds: Obstacles to overcome.

Given time and patience, those with natural visual psychic ability will begin to discern pictures on the surface of the object. This is sometimes called "creative visual imagination" or "imaging," and it may represent past or future events or their symbolic representations. These may appear as only a glimpse upon the inner vision of the interpreter, but remember that there are no hard and fast rules regarding the interpretation of these images. Rely on your own intuition and necessary good judgment when assigning value to these images. Scrying is an erratic art at best, and even the most gifted will find they have good days and bad days, simply because, while it is the least limiting of divinatory practices, it is also the most subjective. There are really only two principles that always apply when scrying: Don't attempt it for other people until you are confident of your ability to do so; and don't attempt crystal-gazing or scrying when you are aware that you are not in the best state—mentally, physically, or emotionally—to do so.

Dice

Using dice as a method of fortune-telling derives from the larger category of numerology, in which numbers are given interpretive significance and are believed to determine a person's basic characteristics, life path, and fortunes according to the numerological values of their date of birth, name, and so on. This particular method dictates that one's fortunes can be determined by the fall of the dice and interpreted according to numerological principles. One of the methods of divination that does not require much in the way of advance preparation or serious study, divination by dice in some of its simpler forms could almost be classified a fortune-teller's game. Others are far more complicated, and there are those who swear by their accuracy. No matter what your view of the practice, though, divination by dice can certainly provide the practitioner with an easy and fascinating introduction to numerology itself. Following are two methods to get you started.

Method 1: To determine the most significant event in your life during the upcoming lunar month, draw a circle about nine inches in diameter on a piece of paper. Concentrating, shake three dice together in your left hand, until your inner voice tells you that they are "ready" to be thrown. Throw the dice, aiming toward the center of the circle. Disregarding any dice that fall outside the drawn circle, total up the numbers thrown and reduce the total to a single-digit number. For example: $6 + 3 + 6 = 15$ and $1 + 5 = 6$. Interpret your findings according to the list below:

0: It is rare that all three dice fall outside the boundaries of the drawn circle, but it has been known to happen. Prepare for the next month to be uneventful in the extreme.

1: The next month will be one filled with good fortune and pleasant and even some unpleasant surprises. Be alert for strokes of unexpected luck, surprising partings, or even the proverbial one-night stand.

2: During the next month you will encounter an event or series of setbacks that will be thoroughly depressing, but you must be aware that everything happens for the best, and the current stormy weather is only a blessing in disguise.

3: Some very exciting surprises await you over the next few weeks; this is a time when you are highly creative and work particularily well with others.

4: Four is the number of Saturn. Circumstances and plans will require personal discipline in order to succeed this month.

5: It's a month to get out there and make some new friends. The contacts you make now will be with you for a long time to come.

6: Unless you are very careful indeed, there is a loss of some kind indicated this month. It could be of monetary, sentimental, or a more abstract value, but this is not the time to be careless or to gamble. Look for news in the mail.

7: Gossip and rumors abound this month, and you may find yourself surprised by the attitude of allies and friends. Take the time to set people straight. It's a confusing time for all kinds of relationships; you may find yourself the object of unrequited love.

8: Check and double check this month, for you are in danger of mishaps and mistakes. It's the kind of month when it is likely that you'll take the blame for your secretary's typos or flub an important presentation because the figures won't add up. Keep a low profile; take a vacation if you can, or otherwise delegate responsibilities to those you can trust.

9: You may, quite unexpectedly, find yourself in the position of having to make decisions about long-term relationships. You could get a proposal, think about divorce, or take a pregnancy test.

Method 2: This is a question-and-answer technique that can provide specific responses to such time-honored areas of human inquiry as, Does X really love me? Should I change jobs? Am I ever going to have any fun again as long as I live? Will I be this poor forever? And so on. Proceed as previously outlined. Throw three dice inside the circle you have drawn on a piece of paper and total up the numbers shown on the dice. This time, though, it isn't necessary to reduce the totals to a single-digit number. Look up the response to your question under the appropriate number and proceed accordingly.

0: There is not enough information available to resolve the matter.

1: A stalemate: Opposing forces are too finely balanced to be able to predict a definite outcome.

3: The next month will decide; ask again in three weeks' time.

4: Generally, yes. Guard against self-absorption.

5: No. You must change your ways in order to change your world.

6: Yes. You have nothing to worry about.

7: Yes, but only with increased self-reliance.

8: Yes, but you must make a sacrifice of some kind first.

9: Perhaps, with persistence and time.

10: This is an unreal problem or question. Ask what you truly mean.

11: Nothing is certain; a matter of chance.

12: Yes—if you are serious.

13: Only if you are cautious.

14: Inwardly, you already know the answer to this question.

15: Behave decisively, but be sure of your facts.

16: Only if you are true to yourself.

17: To get what you want, you must take some risks.

18: Not at the moment. Wait for a sign.

Dominoes

No one is quite sure where the method of divination by dominoes comes from, but it is an easy and undemanding way of telling fortunes, particularly for the novice or beginning diviner. There are two very basic methods used.

Method 1: Use an entire set of dominoes, place face down on a flat surface, and shuffle well. Each person participating in the reading selects one domino, and the numbers on that domino are interpreted as to their relationship to the events of the coming week.

6–6: Signifies a lucky week, during which money may arrive from an unexpected source.

6–5: You are likely to be surprised, particularly with news regarding affairs of the heart and family relationships.

6–4: A week concerning joint financial arrangements, legal matters, or contracts.

6-3: Your social life is about to pick up. Respond to all invitations.

6-2: Embarrassing surprises.

6-1: An old friend will ask for help. Don't make promises you can't keep.

6-Blank: Your friends may behave in an unpleasant way. Be careful of gossip.

5-5: A week of change. You may consider moving or interviewing for a new job.

5-4: Luck is with you; a good week to take a risk or modest gamble.

5-3: Work takes up more of your time than you want, but it will pay off in the end.

5-2: A very exciting week. Visit new places if you can.

5-1: A temporary romance is in the air.

5-Blank: A gloomy week lies ahead. There may be a parting of the ways. Keep your sense of humor.

4-4: A long journey will result in happiness. Accept all invitations, even if they involve trouble or expense.

4-3: An old lover shows up. This could lead to exciting developments. Stay calm.

4-2: A week in which everything improves, especially money matters.

4-1: A week of worry, particularly over finances. Avoid disputes and check your temper.

4–Blank: You may receive unpleasant news; remain cool and aloof despite provocation.

3–3: A week to be involved in other people's problems, whether you like it or not.

3–2: Take no chances; be careful and cautious. This is not your lucky week.

3–1: A mystery will be cleared up.

3–Blank: Don't listen to gossip. Scandal is in the air. This is a week abounding in unfounded rumors, so watch your step.

2–2: A pleasant week, but be careful of jealousy.

2–1: Avoid financial matters if you can. On no account should you borrow or lend money.

2–Blank: Expect annoying delays. Try to remain calm.

1–1: An exciting week. Spend as much time as possible out of doors.

1–Blank: A very boring week indeed. Very dull.

Blank–Blank: The dullest week on record. Things should pick up, however.

Method 2: This is even easier and designed to give a reading of the year to come.

Remove all dominoes with blank halves from the set. Shuffle the remainder and draw three of them, interpreting and combining their meanings as follows:

6–6: Unbelievable good fortune. A very lucky year on all fronts.

6–5: Excellent progress in one's career.

6–4: Luck with money.

6–3: Luck in love.

6–2: A wonderful social life. New friends.

6–1: Much travel; happy vacations.

5–5: Hard work that will pay off. Aspects are generally good.

5–4: Generally prosperous.

5–3: Romance with a colleague.

5–2: Colleagues become friends. Don't push it.

5–1: More work-associated travel.

4–4: A year dominated by financial matters. Watch your pennies and investments.

4–3: Love life proves costly.

4–2: Be careful of frittering away your resources, particularly where friends are involved.

4–1: Don't overspend on luxury items; take a camping trip instead of a tour of the Continent.

* * *

3–3: You may find your true love this year. Clear the decks.

3–2: A year during which progress in career and romance move ahead and are equally balanced.

3–1: Interesting encounters with foreigners or people from a distance.

2–2: Good fortune. Beware of complacency and save for that rainy day.

2–1: A year during which fortunes are made and lost. Be careful when traveling.

1–1: A restless year with some restrictions.

Dowsing (Rhabdoscopy)

Dowsing was originally used to find treasure, mineral deposits, or water hidden underground. Tradition suggests that dowsers cut a hazel wand with a single stroke under the light of the full moon, at a day and hour consecrated to Mercury. The wand was the length of an ordinary walking stick and was carried parallel to the horizon. The dowser's hands were slightly bent under the V-shaped stick, palms turned down toward the ground, and the wand held lightly by the index finger.

If this procedure was followed accordingly, the dowser's wand would turn abruptly toward the earth where the treasure, water, or mineral lay. This procedure proved successful enough to warrant a scientific study in 1910. Undertaken by the British Society of Dowsing, the study proved that a change in muscle tone, measured in electromagnetic waves, takes place in the human body when a person walks over water, strong mineral veins, or stores of metal under the ground.

The dowsing wand can be made of whalebone, hazel, apple, privet, brass, copper, or steel wire; and pendulums can be used in a variation of the method. In fact, many gifted dowsers practice their art in the comfort of their homes using a large-scale map of the area to be dowsed and a pendulum (see "Pendulums" for more information). It is generally agreed that a dowsing wand should be from six inches to a foot long and as thick as one's finger.

Dowsing has not been without its critics. In the early 1800s, Father Malebranch stated that "it is the Devil who makes the wand turn, in order to enrich his slaves in this world, before roasting them in the next." It is interesting to note that the good priest's name, *Malebranch,* roughly translates to "bad stick" in French, which may have been at least some of the basis for his dislike of the practice.

Whatever his feelings on the matter, dowsing is a tried and true method for finding hidden springs prior to sinking wells and for unearthing lost objects. Should you find yourself skeptical, simply try a practice run around your house and then compare your findings with the local utility's map of water mains in the area. To make such an experiment even more interesting, try a forked willow wand. Stroll around your backyard and see what develops. Perhaps you've lost a special ring while out in the garden or an earring at your last barbecue.

The important thing to remember is that when you feel a sudden lurch, your dowsing stick is in working order. Patience, a good attitude, and a sense of adventure will do the rest.

Dreams

The art of dream interpretation operates apart from the more familiar significance applied by psychoanalysts and practitioners of various schools of psychology. There are many books available on dream interpretation: you might want to buy one and keep it by your bed to look up symbols or events portrayed in your dreams when you first wake up in the morning. Ancient dream lore interprets dreams as forecasts of the future of the dreamer or those he or she knows well. The ancients often gave curious warnings. We include here, for the reader's edification, the comments of St. Nicophorus, the patriarch of Constantinople, published for the first time in the ninth century:

"Before you can even hope for the future to be revealed you must learn to know yourself and to dominate your passions and carnal appetites. When you are a master of yourself, if you go to sleep (having first prayed to God) you may see some symbolic images representing future events. But if your belly is loaded with meat, [or] you have drunk more wine than was fitting, you will be obsessed by trivial fantasies, and your spirit will be lost in the realms of darkness.''

Sometimes it is difficult to remember dreams. Keep a dream notebook by your bed and a candle or flashlight in case you wake up in the middle of the night and want to record your dream. Before you go to sleep, relax completely in bed and tell yourself to remember whatever you dream that night. When you wake up in the morning, write down whatever you remember. It is not important that your memories be logical or that they make sense; just write down your impressions. After a week or so, you will find a marked improvement in your ability to remember your dreams. Keep your dream diary for six months, and after awhile you will begin to see patterns emerging in your own unique symbology of dreams.

Remember at all times that a dream means primarily what it means to you, the dreamer. Some dreams may be clairvoyant, some may not. Learn to tell the difference. For instance, if you are under a great deal of stress and anxiety as a result of personal difficulties, your dreams will concern themselves with the psychological aspects of your situation rather than containing future portents and symbols. Never try to interpret your dreams when you are depressed, worried, or anxious. Wait until your mind is clear and you can be objective about what your subconscious is trying to tell you. If you have a dream that you cannot immediately interpret, write down the information and come back to it later.

We include the following traditional interpretations of various dream symbols:

Accidents: Accidents in a dream are symbols of the contrary—that is, they tend to mean the opposite of their usual connotation. To dream of accidents, then, means that happy surprises are in the offing.

Aroma: Breathing an unpleasant aroma because it is close or intimate stands for something within the self and foretells sadness or some kind of affliction.

Animals: This depends on which animal you are dreaming about. To be bitten by a dog means harm from unexpected quarters. Eagles are a god symbol in mythology and mean a warning of danger from above, or from something unknown. See *Birds, Cows, Lions, Vipers, Zoo.*

Babies: A smiling baby foretells good fortune; a crying baby means a disappointment is coming.

Bathing or *Baths:* To take a bath in a

dream is symbolic of a cleansing away of unpleasant influences. If the water is deep, it means that some good fortune is coming your way.

Birds: It depends upon the type of bird that appears in the dream. A cock or rooster, for example, means the realization of hopes. Crows warn of dangerous advice or shameful action. Songbirds mean your troubles will soon be ended. Chickens indicate you lack courage.

Blood: To dream of blood means a friend is going to ask for help. Giving it will be the cause of a lot of worry, but the request should not be refused.

Boats: Change your ways as quickly as possible. Alternatively, you are afraid of change long overdue.

Cows: Cows or oxen mean tactlessness or imprudence and are a warning to be cautious.

Death: Another contrary symbol that portends good news. The same is true for funerals, coffins, et cetera.

Dirt: To be covered with dirt in a dream signifies feelings of humiliation or loss. On the other hand, if you find yourself slogging through the mud in a dream, it means you are involved in something that will prove to be a vain effort.

Eating: The significance of eating dreams

depends upon what is being eaten. A banquet means good news. Eating fish in a dream foretells unlucky turns of events in all your plans. Eating meat means you will enjoy a dubious reward.

Eunuch: A good symbol, indicating that the dreamer has eliminated the struggle between the male and female elements in him or herself.

Falling: A disappointment is in the offing.

Fire: The significance of this dream depends on what is being burned. If you see your house burning, it is a bad sign, and you are materially threatened. If you see a house other than your own burning, it indicates that strength and power are present in your self-awareness. If you dream a part of your body is burned, it is a warning of some scandal which will harm your reputation.

Flying: A caution against being overambitious or working too hard.

Gifts: A very good dream omen. If the dreamer is the giver, it means good fortune is on the way. If you are given a gift in a dream, it means someone is trying to tell you something.

Gold: To dream of gold is a reminder of the adage the "all that glitters is not." It is a warning that special consideration should be taken: Things are not as they seem.

Hair: To dream of hair growing can foretell a minor accident. To dream of losing your hair or of baldness signifies unexpected good fortune. Cutting your hair means that your strength, like Samson's, is diminishing in some way.

Jewels and *Jewelry:* Jewels signify prosperity and beauty. They are a fortunate sign. But to dream you are wearing jewelry—a necklace, for example—can mean you are about to experience some restriction.

Keys: Losing keys means the dreamer should brace him- or herself for trouble. Finding keys indicates a new emotional relationship.

Kissing: Signifies an unexpected gift.

Ladders: Be cautious; you may have false friends.

Laughter: The person who laughs in a dream will cry the next day, and the reverse is also true.

Letters: If you are writing the letters, it is time to take a risk; if you are receiving letters, good news is coming.

Lions: Your enemies are powerful.

Love: To meet a person you love in a dream is a hopeful augury. It indicates that the part of your mind that deals with love is ready for a relationship.

Marriage: Someone else's marriage suggests good fortune on the way. To see your-self being married indicates quarrels with the one you love.

Mirror: Keep your temper. There is a danger of losing a relationship if you don't.

Money: If you find money you can expect to experience something pleasant in the near future.

Moon: Your sex life is about to take a turn for the better.

Nakedness: You have a deep-seated fear of gossip. Pay attention to your secrets; you don't want them exposed.

Numbers: Emotional difficulties are ahead.

Prison: To dream of being in prison is an indication of a forthcoming sexual adventure.

Pursuit: If you are being pursued in your dream, outrunning your problems will do you no good. Face them and they will go away. If you are the pursuer, you are unsure of your goals and priorities. Find out what you are chasing.

Quarrels: An unexpected visitor. Perhaps a guest who will not leave.

Singing or *Music:* Hearing others sing or hearing music in a dream is a sign of prosperity. To play an instrument or hear yourself sing is an indication of setbacks.

Snow: Your problems will be solved by outside sources.

Stairs: To climb stairs means your ambitions will be realized. The higher the stairs, the greater your fortune. Descending stairs is an indication of difficulties to be encountered.

Strangers: Change will occur soon, and your life will never be quite the same.

Vehicle: Automobiles, horses, and carts usually stand for the self: The four wheels or limbs correspond to the four limbs of a human being. If the vehicle is out of control, the dreamer is in danger of losing control of his or her life. A fall could mean either bodily collapse, illness, or simply a sense of failure.

Vipers: Venomous reptiles, snakes, et cetera, represent the image of an enemy and are signs of danger.

Walking: If you walk slowly, it means you will achieve success with difficulty. If you are under a heavy burden as you walk, it foretells oppression and humiliation. If you walk on broken glass, shells, or bones, it signifies you are passing through an insubstantial period in your life—any difficulties are temporary.

Wall: A wall is a sign of solid achievement.

Wine: Spilled wine means an end to your

troubles; drinking wine, on the other hand, means trouble to come.

Zoo: Any dream involving animals or birds in cages means the dreamer should exercise caution. Perhaps there are people working against your interests.

Fire (Pyromancy)

Another form of scrying, divination by fire, or pyromancy, operates on much the same principles outlined elsewhere in these pages. In fact, many diviners find it easier than, say, crystal-scrying, due to the natural, relaxed, and cozy state induced by the the presence of a warm fire.

Fire-diviners use three separate elements to interpret future events: visions seen in the fire itself, those discerned in the smoke, and, finally, visions seen in the ash. Others of still another persuasion swear by the accuracy of those shapes seen hovering in chimney and grate corners, behind the fire itself. Read the section on crystal-gazing to get an initial sense of how fire-scrying is performed. Dim the lights, relax, and allow the mind to wander within as you gaze fixedly at a chosen point. The clouds described in the watery visions of the crystal are more unlikely to appear in this method, but the general principles of interpretation that apply to colors remain the same. There are those who will object—insisting that all fires are yellow and orange—yet anyone who has attempted fire-scrying knows that there are dimensions of color in flame and smoke that go far beyond that kind of protest. Some fire-scryers even insist that a fire gives one the added perspective of seeing oneself in the visions provided by the flames.

For simple answers to yes or no questions, concentrate on the issue at hand and, when you are ready, toss a handful of rosin onto the banked coals. If the coals burst into flame, the answer to your question is yes. If they smoke and go out, the answer is no.

If you have a question pertaining to affairs of the heart, try this method out for fun. On All Souls' Day, place two nuts on the fire side by side, representing the individuals in question. Observe carefully. Do the nuts burn away happily together? Flare up alone? Leap away from each other? Their behavior will give you an indication of the effects of marriage upon each lover named.

Folk Spells

There are thousands of folk spells in the world, whimsical ways to discover facts about the future. Folk spells are not always accurate, and they often tell us more about the people who invented them than about the future, but they are fun to do and they seem to produce results—at least enough to keep them in use.

Many folk spells have to do with weather and its effect on farming communities, whose fortunes were often at the mercy of the elements. In the Highlands of Scotland, old men watched the wind on New Year's Eve carefully. A south wind meant heat and produce, a north wind meant that the coming year would be cold and blustery; west winds indicated a year of heat and milk, and the east wind was fruitful.

New Year's Eve or Day, Halloween, and Midsummer Eve (June 21, eve of the summer solstice) were traditionally the most auspicious times to perform folk spells.

On Halloween, it was recommended that if an unmarried person wanted to see their future husband or wife, they take an apple into an empty room with them. The apple was then sectioned into nine pieces. As the person cut the apple, he or she was to say the names of the Father and the Son. After eating eight pieces with one's back to a mirror, the ninth piece of apple was thrown over the left shoulder. If the querent was quick enough, he or she could look into the mirror and see the future husband or wife coming to take the piece of apple away.

A much less satisfactory method was for a person to go in the Devil's name to a barn and began winnowing grain in secret. If he paid attention, it was a sure bet that he would see his future wife walk into the barn for a moment to watch him.

If a person filled their mouth with water and managed not to swallow it, then went to their neighbor's window and eavesdropped on the conversation, the first name mentioned would be that of their future partner.

Stealing kale or corn stalks was also a good way of finding out the outcome of marriage. It was of the utmost importance that the kale be stolen, however, without the owner of the kale field knowing anything about it. The first stalk a person's hand touched must be pulled. If there was a clump of dirt at the root, the future wife or husband would bring with them money and property. If the querent took home the kale stalk and put it above the door lintel, the first person through the door in the morning would be the husband or wife. If it were put under one's pillow, the dreamer would be sure to dream prophetic dreams.

On Halloween, it was a common occurrence for young women of England, Scotland, and Wales to go to a stream bordering two properties. They then bent down and picked out three stones from the stream, repeating this rhyme:

"I will lift the stone,
As Mary lifted it for her Son,
For substance, virtue, and strength.
May this stone be in my hand
Till I reach my journey's end."

The stones were then put under the pillow while the girl slept, and the girl would be sure to dream of her future, as well as be endowed with the strength and virtues asked for in the rhyme.

Forehead Divination (Metoscopy)

Divination by the forehead is one aspect of the larger discipline of divination by physiognomy. For centuries, people have believed that certain physical types were considered indicative of personality traits; taken in the light of what contemporary diviners know about the laws of genetics, heredity, and so forth, however, much of these early traditions have fallen by the wayside. Consider the old belief, for example, that short, muscular, physical types were thought to be lacking in spirituality, artistic inclinations, and intelligence, as well as being more susceptible to satanic possession, and you get a pretty good idea why this type of reading came under ridicule in the light of modern times.

Yet if our physical characteristics are inherited, there are very few who will deny that the lives we lead can lend a certain cast to those features that is entirely of our own

creation, and it is that aspect to which divination by the forehead truly addresses itself. Remember, too, that in spiritual
tradition, the center of the forehead is the
location of the Third Eye, and perhaps the
reading of that alone is the reason why, of
any type of reading by physiognomy,
forehead-reading continues to survive.

In order to divine by the forehead, mentally divide the face into three sections—the
eyes and forehead, the middle section (nose
and cheekbones), and the mouth and jaw.
The forehead's general size and structure
will indicate general characteristics of an individual's personality, while the lines
etched there will speak of their individual
fortunes.

Type of Forehead	Personality Traits
High and narrow	Narrow minded but has great self-discipline
Broad and square	High energy but lacks sensitivity
Dominant forehead section	Thoughtful; a fine intellect
Rounded middle; narrow temples	Well-balanced personality
Protruberant	Violent tendencies; mediocre mind

Irregular, bumpy	Easily corrupted; a perfidious nature
Short or low	An impulsive nature; strongly verbal

The Lines

Forehead-readers divide the forehead into seven sections, separated by roughly parallel lines that cross horizontally. Each of the seven lines is assigned a planetary ruler, and the visibility or absence of these lines determines the fortunes of the subject. Remember that very few people have all seven lines visible, so the indications for the absence of these lines, as listed below, while traditional in interpretation, may not necessarily be accurate. A prominence of some lines, however, may be seen as an indicator that an individual's characteristics are prominent in those areas of life governed by their planetary ruler. Therefore, someone with a prominent line of Mercury and no line of the Sun or Venus might be seen as someone who favors the intellectual life over the acquisition of wealth or sensual pleasure.

Saturn rules the highest line, just under

the hairline. If this line is very faint, it means that your absence of careful planning will result in misfortune. If strongly marked, it means success through perseverance. If broken in the middle, a life of perpetual ups and downs is indicated. A C-shape on this line indicates someone with an extraordinary memory. A 3-shape appearing on this line foretells an ambush or unforeseen accident, while a V-shape means exile or some kind of separation from loved ones.

Jupiter's line lies just below that of Saturn. If it is very faint it indicates a flighty nature, someone more or less at the mercy of chance. If this line is very strong, it indicates material security and wealth. If broken, you will be compromised in the future. A 3-shape on this line is an indicator of certain success.

Mars rules the next line. If it is clearly pronounced, the individual is a risk-taker or, in some cases, pugnacious. If it is faint, broken, or nonexistent, it indicates pliability, timidity, or lack of strong convictions, respectively. A 3-shape indicates someone with a fine future in the armed services, but the threat of imprisonment looms ahead. A V-shape also indicates success in the military.

The *Sun* rules the line that roughly divides the forehead in half. If clearly marked, it indicates a love of luxury and the finer things in life. If uneven or broken, it means someone who will stop at nothing to succeed—or someone in whom kindness and cruelty coexist in an unpredictable fashion. If very faint, this person has a big ego. If a 3-shape appears anywhere on this line, it means the person will lose a fortune. A V-shape means someone who must leave his birthplace in order to succeed.

The line of *Venus,* if clearly marked, indicates an ardent and passionate nature. If broken, it means a tendency to excesses of the senses or a struggle between reason and emotion. An S-shape on this line shows someone inclined towards clandestine relationships, while a 3-shape presages an unfortunate marriage through infidelities. A C-shape here indicates dangers that arise from amorous adventures.

Mercury rules the next line; if it is very strong, it indicates a fine ability to communicate and a good imagination. If broken, a tendency to always dominate the conversation is indicated, a person with whom you can't get a word in edgewise. If it is faint, it indicates a thoughtful but uncommunicative type. A cross on this line indicates the possibility of persecution, especially for writers. A C-shape on this line shows a mind always able to see both sides of a question, though perhaps poor judgment. A figure like a 3 indicates someone who will enjoy a fine future in a religious order or the law.

The line of the *Moon* is just above the brow ridge. If very deeply marked, it shows a melancholy nature. If broken, it reveals someone who is up and down with manic regularity. If very faint, it tells of someone uninvolved in life. A 3-shape here means a violent death, while a C-shape on the line or between the brows indicates someone of an irritable nature.

Other than the principal lines and their markings, some popular traditions regarding particular formations and shapes of secondary lines are indicated below.

A single horizontal line dividing the forehead with a dip in the middle is a sure indicator of someone who will be famous within his or her lifetime. Two lines that rise up from the bridge of the nose indicate a possessive nature with a tendency to jealousy, and there are some who believe that if these lines are double, it is a sign of someone who will be imprisoned at some point for crimes of passion. A single line between the brows, on the other hand, foretells a life of loneliness and avarice, or someone to whom wanting proves better than having. Three S-shapes together was thought by the ancients to be a certain indicator of death by drowning, whereas a P-shape appearing anywhere on the forehead was a sign of the love of good food and drink. A square or triangle that appears anywhere on the forehead is a sign of money easily gained; when it appear in the center of the forehead or on the line of the Sun, it indicates someone who has trouble holding onto their money—a spendthrift. Circles that appear anywhere on the forehead are a sign of ill health, but if found on the line of the Moon, they're an indicator of blindness in old age. Y-shapes, too are signs of poor health, but if they appear anywhere on the line of Mars, they presage some disease of the joints—arthritis, rheumatism, or even gout. An M-shape that appears anywhere in the lines of the forehead is a more fortunate sign that foretells a peaceful (if somewhat mediocre) life and death in one's sleep.

Genies

Belief in supernatural beings—inferior to the gods but able to affect the fortunes of gardens, woodlands, mountain areas, and the people who inhabit them—has persisted despite all attempts by civilization and organized religion to weed them out of folk culture and primitive superstition. The general perception of these beings resembles the Arabic and Persian idea of *peris*, who are described as possessing a quality of lightness and insubstantiality not found in humans. Generally thought to be creatures of the four elements—water, fire, earth, and air—genies, brownies, elves, sidhe, fairies, and the like fly through the air, appear erratically to human observers, inhabit streams, flowers, and trees, and, in Northern European countries, can be petitioned for certain things, although most fairy lore has to do with negating their effects on the unsuspecting. The French call them *fées*, the Irish call them *sidhe* or *leprechauns,* in Wales they are known as the *Tylwyth-Teg,* and in Germany and Scandinavia they are known as *stille-volk, kobbolds, alfen,* or *nokke.*

The Gauls believed that their druids, once they were run out of the country by the Romans, fled to Great Britain. It was the souls of inferior druids who eventually became fairies, suspended between earth and heaven until the day of judgment. Children in the Middle Ages were taken to halls or stone configurations sacred to fairies upon their birth, whereupon the fairies endowed the child with gifts that foretold the kind of life the child was to have.

Because these elemental spirits were so insubstantial, most humans saw only the effects of their passing. Shepherds and cowherders or those forced to spend long periods outside in the dark heard fairies pass closely by them, their identity betrayed by a sharp whistling sound. It was considered very dangerous to speak to them. If one did, the consequences could be as varied as prophetic visions, traveling far distances through the air, being thrown to the ground and killed, or, worst of all, entrapment. When fairies passed in the night they left traces of their passing on the ground. Sometimes the grass seemed parched yellow, and those with sharp enough eyes could pick out the outlines of tiny footprints. Other times, the grass became a deeper green than the surrounding vegetation. Fairies were thought to be responsible for mysterious human disappearances and for playing ill-timed and bad-tempered tricks on cattle, livestock, and inhospitable inhabitants of houses.

Elves, brownies, and other elementals were thought to be especially active on Fridays. They had an aversion to iron and water, were easily offended, and particularly disliked activities related to weddings or sharpening iron objects on a Friday. Tragedy could sometimes be averted if a person had the foresight to mutter "A blessing on their journeying and traveling, this is Friday and they will not hear us." Nevertheless, it was of great importance not to irritate a sidhe on Friday because it was on Fridays that these spirits could kill with a single breath.

Crossroads and full moons had also to be avoided, on Halloween in particular. In the British Isles, fairies seemed to make it a perverse habit to reside underneath houses and wreak havoc on those who lived within. Yet contact with the little people did not have to have unfortunate results. Anyone who complied with the creatures' wishes, however

absurd, and who could at the same time resist laughing at the spirits could count on
their help in disastrous situations.

It was said among the Welsh that once
everyone had gone to bed for the night, pro-
viding the floor was swept, the hearth
cleaned and water drawn for morning, fairies would come and frolic, leaving at day-
break with the gift of a gold coin on the
hearth for the trouble the inhabitants had
gone to the night before. But if a housewife
found a log burned to ashes when she got
up early, she was warned not to curse or
make the sign of the cross—the burning log
would immediately become a mess of cin-
ders.

Although genies, fairies, sidhe, and
brownies would often go out of their way to
prosper a household, once they were cursed
or driven away, they left in their wake such
destruction and havoc as would cause
everyone to wish they were dead—which
would not happen, unless the death were
lingering and particularly unpleasant.

German *stille-volk* never spoke. It was
said that every great German house had its
familiar, who accompanied each member of
the household and behaved in much the
same way as a guardian angel, engineering
good fortune where possible and averting
daily annoyances. If, however, a tragedy

was so great that there was nothing to be done about it, the *stille-volk* would often appear and try to warn the unsuspecting victim by setting up a weeping and moaning all around the house.

Stille-volk bore a close resemblance to British spirit-rappers or ghost lights, both of which appeared to warn of a particularly grisly and protracted death.

It is interesting to note that the more one proceeded north, the more questionable the behavior of fairies and the like became. Northern spirits, in particular, seemed to resist change and were blamed for such things as transporting entire churches away from places deemed unsuitable. The first night of the new year seemed to be a particularly active time for these spirits, and it was then that they were most prone to reveal the future if they were not offended. Upon occasion, they would appear as unworldly dogs or wild animals, and afforded protection to those who had left them milk and fruit or left a light in the window to help guide their paths.

Offended elves and sprites particularly liked to vent their spleen on horses and often tormented the creatures into bloody frenzies if bits of cheese were not left around the stable. They would also spoil wine and cause general havoc and, at their very worst, lead the unsuspecting to horrible deaths.

Not many folk spells survive for getting information out of fairies or genies, but we have included some that are to be performed on Halloween night.

If a person throws a shoe over his house by the toe, its position on the other side of the house will tell the person who threw the shoe the direction in which he will shortly head off on a journey. If the shoe is found with the sole facing the sky, misfortune is in the making.

Eggwhite, dropped slowly into a glass of springwater, will indicate how many children the querent will have. To seek the counsel of the little folk, unmarried women should take balls of thread, after first crossing a wall, to a kiln or a outhouse. After throwing the ball of thread over the wall, they must call out loud, "Who is at the end of my rope?" If the spell is successful, something will pull the end of the string and shout out the name of her future husband.

If a young man goes to a well to the south of his house, drenches his shirt in the water, pulls off his shirt and sets it out before the fire to dry, the spirits are thought to transport his future wife to the scene. She will appear to turn his shirt in the middle of the night, and the young man is almost sure to see her—if he manages to stay awake that long.

If a person washes his or her feet in a bowl of water and leaves it out overnight to attract the fairies, he will, in exchange for this courtesy, be able to see the color of his or her future mate's hair by putting a handful of burning coal in the water in the morning.

Herbal Divination

The use of herbs to enchance the diviner's clairvoyant powers is as old as the fortune-telling arts themselves. Herbal tradition generally employs herbs and oils as an adjunct to other divining methods, rather than a method in and of itself. Still, one or two systems involving the interpretation of symbols drawn in powdered or crumbled herbs are still practiced. Listed below are some hints and methods for the use of herbs in divinatory rituals and to enchance one's clairvoyant powers. Some of these herbs may be available in the spice section of the supermarket; others may be harder to locate—try health-food stores, herb specialists, and mail-order sources.

Seer's Incense

An all-purpose incense formula to be used while reading Tarot, crystals, et cetera, may be made as follows: Mix equal parts of gum mastic, patchouli, juniper, sandalwood, and cinnamon. During the time of the moon's increase, moisten these herbs with a few drops of ambergris oil. Burn a small amount before proceeding with a reading to enhance the Sight.

Scrying Incense

To strengthen the powers of a crystal or glass bowl used for scrying, rub it prior to a reading with mugwort leaves. During the gazing interval, be sure to burn a mixture comprised of equal portions of mugwort and wormwood, to enhance and clarify your visions.

Clairvoyance Vapor

This recipe is probably as old as the witch's cauldron, but there's no need to run out and invest in a huge iron pot, a black dress, or a bad haircut in order to make it work. As long as you have a stove and a medium-sized saucepan, you can proceed with enthusiasm.

Fill a pan with springwater (bottled will do nicely), and let it simmer over medium heat until it steams. Add to the water a handful of bay laurel (bay) leaves, a handful of mugwort, and a handful of cinquefoil. Cover the pot and allow the mixture to steep for three minutes. Turn off the heat and remove the pot to a comfortable location. Remove the lid and inhale the vapors deeply, breathing from the diaphragm. (Be careful! Don't lean so close that you burn yourself!) Still all thoughts and hold your mind quiet. You will begin to experience psychic impressions very shortly. To induce clairvoyant dreams, inhale the brew just before going to bed.

Herb Scrying

On a Wednesday evening, crumble together an equal portion of dried patchouli, mugwort, and wormwood until it is the texture of fine crumbs. Pour it onto a mirror. Close your eyes and draw at random with the index finger of your left hand, until you feel it is time to stop. Open your eyes and interpret the symbols that appear.

The Herbal Pillow

To induce clairvoyant dreams, you may want to try this popular nineteenth-century method. Sew a pillow, roughly nine inches square, and stuff it with a mixture of the following: bay leaves, rose petals, rosemary, mint, and cloves. Sleep on it for several nights in a row and you will begin to have visions in your dreams.

As a final note, the use of oil of anise has long been considered invaluable to the development of clairvoyant powers. Use it in your bath, or annoint yourself on the temples, neck, and breast prior to any divinatory reading.

Key Divination
(Kleidoscopy)

Divination by key is practiced in Russia, where its use is generally tied to material gains and losses. For example, if you suspect that someone is a thief or responsible for the loss of a particular object, write his or her name on a slip of paper. Fold up the paper and place it under a key that is attached to a Bible or Testament. The book, key, and paper are then placed in the hands of a young virgin, and the diviner murmurs the suspect's name over and over, asking at the same time that the truth be revealed. If the paper moves, you have found your thief. If the paper remains motionless, the person is proved innocent.

Keys are also thought to be able to discern hidden treasures. In another method, a key that has been attached to a ring is placed in the Bible, at the opening page of the Gospel of St. John. The ring, however, should remain outside the pages. Close the book and slip the index finger of your left hand through the ring. Concentrate intensely on a number of likely hiding places. If the ring moves on your finger, look for treasure in the place you have just named. If the ring does not move, you have not yet thought of the treasure's hiding place.

I Ching

The I Ching is an oracle book. It has been said that consulting it is like carrying on a conversation with a witty, urbane, and extremely fair-minded uncle who travels a great deal and is well versed in the lessons of nature. But, like an uncle who has a great deal of experience, the I Ching will not tolerate silly or repetitious questions and, just for the fun of it, will answer questions from another or even opposite perspective if the querent's questions are ill formed or unclear. When consulting the I Ching, it is therefore important to be as specific as possible. For this reason, it is best to write your question down on a piece of paper first and make absolutely sure that your question is clearly phrased. For instance, if you are asking a question about a business venture and your question runs along the lines of "What will be the outcome of this situation?" the I Ching is not adverse to recommending a course of action that will prove to work out perfectly for the other party involved. Nevertheless, it can be a brilliant and useful divinatory tool for those who are of a thoughtful bent or for those faced with complex problems. On the other hand, if your current questions are simple, yes-or-no type conundrums, perhaps another method would be best for the moment.

There are many versions of the I Ching. We recommend that if this form of divination appeals to you, you buy one of them and spend some time reading it before you begin your inquiries. It takes some time to get used to the symbols and word pictures. Those that are not taken from nature are taken from daily Chinese life so ancient that its oriental symbolism is often unwieldy even for modern Chinese. It is difficult to follow advice, for example, which recommends that you observe the tiger when you have never seen a tiger except in an environmentally controlled zoo.

The I Ching will not tell you what will happen in the future. As is the habit of most oracles, it will describe the situation in which you have found yourself. Then it will suggest behavior or a course of action, given your situation. You yourself must decide what you want to do. The future is not written in stone, and any decision of yours can have the power to change your lifepath in limitless ways. For this, the I Ching does not bear any responsibility, nor should it.

The I Ching has evolved into its present state from texts attributed to the twelfth-century Chinese ruler King Wen. Originally, it was based on a system of divination venerated by Taoists and Confucianists alike and was not intended for use by any but intellectuals, spiritual advisors, and military leaders. Since then, the text has evolved and been expanded to become the I Ching in use today.

If one consults the I Ching with an open mind, its advice is often uncannily accurate, despite its sometimes obscure references. When working with a text, make sure you read the hexagram slowly and allow it to speak to you, rather than imposing your own wants and desires onto the symbolism presented.

The advice given by the I Ching is meant to allow a person to behave in such a way that enables him or her to influence the future instead of being blown about by every problem or difficult circumstance confronting them. Therefore, when phrasing your questions to the I Ching, it is best to ask questions like "What is the nature of my current financial situation?" rather than a question like "Will I win the lottery on Wednesday?"

In order to consult the oracle, you must concentrate on a specific question and create a *hexagram*. A hexagram is a figure with six lines. Traditionally, hexagrams were obtained by casting yarrow stalks. This later evolved into using Chinese coins, dice, or even regular coins. You can research and use any method, but for the beginner, it is easiest to use coins.

Concentrate on the question at hand. Write it down to make sure it is specific. Take three coins and toss the coins six times. Each time, write down the throw. Tails are given a value of 3, heads of 2. Add up the number of each throw and record it on a piece of paper. For example, three tails equal the number 9, two heads and a tail equal 5. Draw an unbroken line for every odd number, a broken line for every even number. The only exceptions are what are called moving lines—that is, three heads or three tails, or the number 9 or the number 6. Moving lines signify that the situation is changing. To discover the nature of the change, simply construct a hexagram, substituting the moving line's opposite. For example, three tails or 9 equals an unbroken but moving line. Construct another hexagram using a broken line in the space where the unbroken line was generated by the number 9 and look up the interpretation for that as well. Some versions of the I Ching explore the nature of moving lines in other ways, and if you are interested, you may research these in more detail on your own. But for beginners, the method listed above is by far the most practical.

To discover the I Ching's interpretation of your question, use the chart on the next page. Find the first three lines of your hexagram in the top row and match it with the second three lines of your hexagram seen along the outside row on the left. Find the number on the chart where the two halves meet and read the interpretation listed under that number.

Upper→Half / ↓Lower Half	CH'IEN	CHEN	K'AN	KEN	K'UN	SUN	LI	TUI
CH'IEN	1	34	5	26	11	9	14	43
CHEN	25	51	3	27	24	42	21	17
K'AN	6	40	29	4	7	59	64	47
KEN	33	62	39	52	15	53	56	31
K'UN	12	16	8	23	2	20	35	45
SUN	44	32	48	18	46	57	50	28
LI	13	55	63	22	36	37	30	49
TUI	10	54	60	41	19	61	38	58

Interpretation of the Hexagram

1: This is the hexagram of creative power. Now is the time to be bold without being reckless. Press forward, but direct your energies wisely.

2: Despite the confusion around you, persist and endure. There are obstacles around you, but refrain from acting in a willfull manner. Keep your mind open to the advice of those close to you.

3: This is a time in which you are changing in ways that are yet unformed. You may be experiencing new desires, new tastes, or confusion. This is not a time to act; allow more time for development while you accept the changes within you. Talk over things with outsiders; learn what you can.

4: Are you asking what you want to know? It may be that you are asking foolish or insincere questions, or simply that you are lacking in experience. Look for a teacher. If you are a teacher, it means that your students may doubt you. Discipline yourself or ask again if this hexagram does not make sense to you.

5: Wait for strength in the face of difficulty. You may be in danger. Nothing is under your control; bide your time and wait out your difficulties. Keep a low profile and look for the truth within. Eventually all will be well.

6: This is a time for caution; carefully consider all the factors in your situation and don't burn any bridges behind you. You may need them later. Do not openly confront things, even if you know you are in the right.

7: There is a time for thought and a time for action as well as a time for both. If you act without thinking, you will not achieve what you desire. If you think without action, it means nothing. Do not attempt to organize or mobilize those around you unless it is to a higher cause.

8: This is the hexagram of connectedness. Know that no action is independent; no ambition or course exists outside of society. Join with others. You must give before you can receive. In some instances, this hexagram can indicate the advisability of a second query—your answer may be "connected" to another question.

9: A time to strive and satisfy yourself with small successes. You may feel blocked by forces larger than yourself. Put aside your larger plans for the moment; minor triumphs have merit, too. Be gentle and responsive to the needs of others.

10: The present situation is very difficult because you are faced with problems that seem to have no end, let alone a satisfactory conclusion. Be fearless and bold and treat the situation with as much humor as you can muster, and you will achieve what you desire.

11: Excellent fortunes in love and marriage. Extreme blessings—peace of mind, success, and prosperity, especially as it concerns the personal life.

12: Stagnation. Nothing is reasonable.

Promises will not be kept, and it may be a time to "hide your light under a bushel," for the moment. Be self-reliant and do not attempt to influence others.

13: This is the hexagram of the family. Refrain from making secret agreements. Just as the family operates, everyone has a task—use each person's special abilities to contribute to the whole. Begin new projects in groups but not as an individual.

14: Strokes of unexpected good fortune may result in success and the spotlight. Good for personal and professional relationships and for artists, this indicates great success. Avoid excesses of pride.

15: This is the hexagram of modesty. Do not boast of your achievements; avoid extremes. This is a time when the underdog will triumph, when you will see the truth in the expression "pride goeth before the fall." Be open to new experiences.

16: A time to motivate others through your enthusiasm. Find ways to get others to do what you want through kindness and joy rather than subterfuge. Consider how music inspires the heart through harmony—be harmonious socially, emotionally, and spiritually, and you will inspire others to your objectives.

17: Lie low; circumstances around are uncontrollable. Serve others, remain adaptable, and success will follow.

18: You are overwhelmed by grave difficulties that may not be your fault. Pay attention to detail. The original text of the I Ching recommends three days of contemplation before any action is taken. Be alert to change; the situation could regress or decay if you are not careful.

19: This hexagram represents the coming of spring. You can begin anything you desire—new relationships, new projects, and ventures. Remember, though, that spring is brief and passes quickly. A time of inner growth.

20: The hexagram of contemplation. Contemplate, rest, and master your world. Experience people and ideas fully. Others are watching you; you may reveal yourself inadvertently. You create your world through your perceptions.

21: The hexagram of reform. A situation has developed that is at cross-purposes to your ambitions. The obstacle must be sought, reformed, and eliminated. Your problems will not miraculously vanish. Look inside yourself to determine if illusion, rationalization, or poor habits have usurped control of your judgment and thinking. Justice will be done.

22: You are in a state of grace. Examine

your environment with this extraordinary point of view and you will receive a vision of the possible perfection in the world. Success in human affairs is indicated through tradition and ceremony. Be earnest and idealistic, but know that these are not the qualities that give rise to a permanent situation.

23: There is no advantage now in moving toward a goal. You may feel that inferior people are on the rise and that their power is growing. There is nothing for a person of integrity to do but wait. Things will naturally improve in their own time. If possible, use this time to be generous and supportive of those dear to you.

24: You are repeating a familiar cycle in your life. Be alert for the paths that lead to renewed growth. Old friends or old relationships may reappear now. This will require a decision of some kind; use this time as an opportunity for self-knowledge. You are exiting a phase.

25: The hexagram of innocence. Align yourself to the flow of the cosmos without judgment. Careful plans may end in difficulty and confusion. Examine your motives; they may be the cause of your troubles. Put aside your goals and purposes and do not aspire to reward. Act with innocence and react to situations spontaneously.

26: Direct your potential energies to society rather than personal gain. Now is the time to work toward the fulfillment of a cause or ideology with great success. Concentrate on worldly achievement. Cultivate useful connections. Personal relationships could blossom overnight. View your feelings in the light of history to attain insight.

27: Nourish others but be sure they are worthy of your support. If there are difficulties in your relationships, examine the quality of what you give to others. Exercise discipline over your thoughts, and cultivate constructive opinions and attitudes in order to properly nourish yourself and those around you. Avoid excessive indulgence.

28: The current situation is weighted with a great many considerations. The air is full of ideas, possibilities, and ponderous decisions, and all of it is important, serious, and meaningful. A time when matters come to a head. Look for an avenue of escape. Carefully evaluate all the things affecting you; you will need your wits about you. Have a goal in mind. Rely on the resilience of your character to see you through this crisis with confidence and courage. Remember, action must be taken now.

29: You must accustom yourself to an objective view of the situation. Learning from danger creates confidence. Do not attempt to avoid confrontation; meet and overcome it through correct behavior. Be resolute. Do not compromise what you believe to be right. Integrity is the key to surmounting the danger around you.

30: Join with your opposite and you will achieve synergy. Now is the time when you can enlighten others. Align your desires with those of a loved one. Examine your relationships. Are you working with synergy or against one another? If pressures mount, keep your temper. Work quietly and diligently with others to alleviate difficulties.

31: The hexagram of attraction. You are experiencing a magnetism that is beyond a superficial desire. It is a fortunate time to marry, start a family, or influence others. You are in a position of power that must be expressed through an attitude of service like a lover woos his beloved.

32: This hexagram advises a time of continuing. Perpetuate and renew your situation to find happiness. Do not usurp tradition. Not a time to change for the sake of change. Personal relationships develop comfortably within the structure of enduring social institutions. Continuing speaks to the secret of eternity.

33: Hostile forces are advancing. Retreat is the correct course; by retreat, success will be achieved. Protect your light from the forces of darkness; you cannot win the war right now. Do not allow vengeance to cloud your judgment. Sever lines of communication. Withdraw intellectually and emotionally. Do not attempt to compete with forces beyond your control; it is only a phase.

34: Great power is a reward and a test. All of your actions have significant influence on others now. It is important to act responsibly in this position of power. You will find yourself the center of attention. Improve relations with others and implement good works. Those around you will look to you for leadership. Do not deviate from tradition. You can afford to be at your most benevolent now.

35: An expansive period where your ideas are best put to use in service to others. Your suggestions will have great impact. Wonderful avenues of communication and mutual accord will open for you now. You and your loved ones are now unified; foster your altruism.

36: Censorship. Forces will threaten convictions and attainment of your goals and desires. You are not in a powerful position now. Step into the background and conceal your feelings. Appear to accept your difficulties but do not lose sight of principles. If necessary, you can influence others through subterfuge and intrigue. Hide your feelings but maintain your convictions.

37: Do not hesitate to ask advice of others. Be aware of timing. Enrich your life by adhering to roles based on natural affection and respect for others. Rely on impulse in relationships to suggest your appropriate role. Know your inner strength and authority but be careful of your words.

38: You are experiencing an inner duality that results in indecision. Try to understand the divergent forces within you and concentrate on small achievements now. Great progress is possible but only after the existing polarity is overcome. Great ambitions must wait for a more supportive climate.

39: The hexagram of obstacles. Obstacles you encounter now are part of the path you have chosen. Consider the example of a stream. When the water meets an obstacle, it pauses and builds up strength until the obstacle no longer blocks its way. Rely on others. It is an excellent time to hire those who will help you, or to join forces with others. Be conscientious in social matters. Do not be your own worst enemy.

40: Storms release tension; they clear the air of mistakes and resentments. Be decisive and act without hesitation. Try to return the situation to normal. If something is blocking progress, resolve that issue now. Do not seek retribution or vengeance; your concerns should lie in returning your affairs to a regular pattern. Liberation can replace anxiety. Put the past behind you and your spirit will be refreshed.

41: The hexagram of decline. Simplify your life and concentrate on inner development. Do not rely on your instincts or passions now. There may be material loss, division, or difficulty in communication with loved ones. Do not overreact emotionally.

42: Increase. All undertakings will succeed now, even if they are difficult or dangerous. Make the best of things, for this extraordinary period will not last. Take time to rid yourself of negative forces. Resist self-indulgence and trust your feelings of joy and well-being.

43: You may feel oppressed now but remain resolute in your goals and desires. Resist compromising your principles and speak the truth under any circumstances, even if it means risk. Make sure that the corruption you are fighting does not exist within you. The best way to fight evil is by making energetic progress in good.

44: Things are not what they seem. Guard against inferior allies. Directly confront issues that are important to you. If you do not, you may squander your resources. Be suspicious of new friends or contacts and exercise self-discipline. Do not let inferior people use your power.

45: The hexagram of coming together. You may find yourself in a group that is coming together, either as a leader or a follower. Do everything you can to promote moral harmony. Good fortune may result from sacrifice. Do not be indecisive. If you are prepared for trouble, trouble can be averted.

46: You are carried along by the tides of good fortune, as long as you are willing to adapt yourself to circumstance. Your social status may be upgraded now, and your emotional environment is sure to be supportive. Discipline yourself for long-lasting results.

47: You are surrounded by danger. Keep your sense of humor. Do not let circumstances break your spirit; you will have great influence on the world around you now. Don't say things you don't mean. There is nothing you can do but remain true to yourself.

48: Be intuitive about the motives of those people around you. Consider what might cause them to behave in negative ways. Shortsightedness will bring misfortune. This hexagram applies to social organizations and structures as well as the individual. Do not be a slave to convention.

49: The hexagram of revolution. Great and far-reaching changes are operative now. Not everyone is called to revolution; it must be undertaken only with the support of those around you and only at the correct time. Your personal relationships may require change, but be careful that these are not merely the result of your changing perspective.

50: This is a time to realign yourself spiritually. Destiny may have overtaken you. You may experience revelation of a higher being or inner truth. If you harmonize with what you see, success will be yours. Remain humble and express your new knowledge through service. You may want to toss the coins again in order to more clearly discern where you stand in the order of things.

51: Respect the power of nature. Its forces are promoting new growth. You may find yourself in the midst of sudden and astonishing change. Once this situation has passed, you will be able to experience great joy. Maintain your composure and practice tranquillity and poise. New confidence is born of great change.

52: The hexagram of centering. Retreat within yourself and center your being. Live harmoniously in the present. This is a time for rest and acting in harmony with the universal law.

53: Gradual growth. You have the opportunity to make lasting changes but only if you recognize that progress now will be slow and methodical. Ignore criticism, persevere with calm, and remember to nurture that which is truly important.

54: This is not a good time to be creative. Strengthen your inner vision and don't assert yourself. Function in a subordinate role and make long-range plans.

55. The hexagram of abundance. You are now at the height of your powers—emotionally, financially, socially, or politically. Do not be afraid to let go. This period will be followed by a period of some decline, but the achievements you make now will sustain you. No one can be king of the mountain forever. Use this time to discover as much about yourself as you can.

56: Do not drag out or belabor your difficulties now. You are only passing through. Be humble and defenseless; this is not a permanent situation. Be cautious with those around you: You may be a moving target, because your successes of the past may have left you without protection. Make no long-term commitments; watch, learn, and be true to yourself.

57: Prepare yourself for slow, relentless

efforts. This situation can only be changed gradually. Be gentle and inconspicuous and improve your relationships with those around you. Keep long-term goals in mind and concentrate on your emotional and physical health. Concentration is of great importance now.

58: Social events are highlighted; use this opportunity to support others. Your relationships will improve dramatically if you are empathetic and communicate clearly. Don't be afraid of your emotions; talk about them openly. Success will come easily if it is based on true joy.

59: Avoid rigid thinking and isolation from others. Learn to be a peacemaker. There are things for you to do within your community or social environment. If you are involved in the arts, do not rely on eccentric methods of communication. Make sure that you appeal to the masses.

60: Watch your money. Do not be excessive. Stick to your budget. Accept people for who they are. Don't tell others how to think, what to do, or where to get off. You don't know everything.

61: It is of the utmost importance that you clearly understand others. You may be placed in a position to judge people now, and you ought to use your responsibilities wisely. Do not fight the situation in which you find yourself; be accepting. Your insight and experience could enrich your life immeasurably now.

62: Pay attention. This is not a time for change. Be alert to subtleties; watch your money and your tongue. Learn humility. Pride may keep you from important insights.

63: Success has a life of its own, but do not let this lull you into complacency. Consider a pot of boiling water: If the heat is too great, the water boils over and puts out the fire. Strive for balance; recognize when things are going a little too well and so avert moments of danger.

64: An exciting time, but be wary. Conditions are difficult. Wait until a more auspicious time for action. Achievement of your goals has opened up an entirely new frontier. Learn more about it before going off on any adventure.

Natural Occurrences

There are many diviners who believe that signs of the future are all around us and that no special equipment or method is required to know what is to come, only an ability to read the natural signs the Creator has provided us. As might be expected, reading the weather and other assorted natural phenomena provides the enquirer with information that is rather nonspecific, but it can nevertheless prove an interesting and informative pastime, particularly if you keep a record of the predictions you have made based on natural phenomena and decide for yourself on the accuracy of the method. Many of these beliefs grew out of a tradition of agriculture, and the modern diviner may find them less than useful, but they do, nevertheless, have a basis in tradition, and we include them for that purpose.

Predicting the Weather

People in the Ozarks believe that if a rooster crows persistently just before nightfall, there will be a soaking rain the next day.

Southern American hillfolk maintain that if you count the number of foggy days in August, you can predict the number of snows the following winter.

If a cat eats grass or the fire pops more than three times in an evening, rain or snow is on the way.

The number of stars that shine within the moon's circle are the same as the number of days before the next rain.

If the bark on the north side of a birch tree bursts during the summer, the following winter is sure to be hard.

This one is for citydwellers: If you see a pigeon washing itself, rain is on the way.

If smoke floats to the west, rain is coming; if it floats to the south, there will be a bad storm.

If it thunders on a certain date in December, it will frost the same day in May.

If the animals have heavy pelts, hard winter is on the way.

On whatever date of the month the first snow falls, that is the number of snows that winter.

Good and Bad Fortune

If a hen lays a dwarfed or misshapen egg, it is to be thrown over the barn roof backwards. The egg will carry any bad luck with it.

If you transplant parsley, you are sure to have bad luck.

It is luckiest to fell trees at the wane of the moon. If you wish them to sprout again, fell them during the moon's increase.

A German proverb states that if there are high winds between Christmas and New Year's, the trees of an orchard will "copulate" and there will be a bountiful harvest.

If a tree will not bear fruit, place iron and stones at its base and its fertility will increase.

If you name a first child after one of its parents, the child will have poor luck in life.

If a child is born with a caul, it will have the power of prophecy.

A baby born after its father's death will have occult powers.

Listening to the Wind

Witches were at one time persecuted for this sort of thing, but listening to the voices of the wind is nevertheless an easy and relaxing method of divination, particularly if you are a sound-oriented individual. Find a peaceful location in a woods or park, far removed from any noisy distractions, such as the sounds of traffic or children playing. Lie down on the ground in a comfortable spot beneath some trees. Feel the sensations of the breeze as it plays gently over your body. Once you are completely relaxed, let your consciousness join with the sounds of the wind, freeing your mind to rise and fall with the rush and murmur of the leaves. You will be surprised to find that you may hear voices; these are the whispers of the wind. Many feel these voices to be important messages from beyond the limits of the conscious mind. Naturally, this method is one that relies heavily on a person's intuition and the ability, as it were, to temporarily suspend disbelief. Nonetheless, you may be surprised by the accuracy of what you hear.

Oracles

Strictly speaking, the use of oracles must be considered as distinct from the other divinatory arts. Whether the oracle used is a book, like the Bible or the I Ching, or a system derived from a source, as the runes have been derived from the Norse alphabet, an oracle is to be used primarily as a tool for meditation. Oracles do not make predictions, and they will not tell the reader the future; they only strive to serve as illuminators of the querent's present situation. Oracles serve as teachers and should be used as such. They're reminders that every soul is on a journey, that growth is a constant process, that no outcome or future is predetermined, that no destiny is assured. We look to oracles and oracle books for wisdom, because these are the places in which the wisdom of our collective unconscious sometimes resides. Yet the oracles should not and cannot be used, in the literal sense, to "tell fortunes." The oracles, whatever their traditional nature or origin, can prove invaluable in the individual's search for enlightenment, yet they are not, and should never be treated as, a game.

Ouija Boards

Almost everyone is familiar with the famous Ouija board, the "Mystifying Oracle" created by William Fuld and first patented in this country by the Parker Brothers Company, of Salem, Massachusetts. An all-time best seller in game, book, and toy stores, the Ouija board is readily available and easy for the novice diviner to use, either alone or with others.

Basically, the system has two components—an alphabet board and a planchette. The board is placed either on a table or upon the knees of the player or players, who then place their fingers lightly upon either side of the planchette until the instrument begins to spell out answers to their inquiries. Like many forms of divination, what exactly makes this method work is unknown. Perhaps the movement is the result of electromagnetic impulses generated by the players themselves, or perhaps it is a means, depending upon the psychic ability of the querents, of contacting spirits from the other side. Perhaps it is simply a tool for contacting the individual unconscious; no one can say with any certainty. What is certain is that many people have enjoyed themselves while deriving useful information from the use of a Ouija or similar board.

To use the board effectively, use the following methods and precautions.

Initially, use the board with another person, preferably someone with whom you can be said to have a rapport. Until you are well versed with the board as a divinatory tool, it will be difficult to work it alone. People of wildly divergent energy patterns can rarely work the planchette successfully. Keep an open mind and approach the board with the same serious intent as you would any other method of divination.

Concentrate upon a question or upon summoning a presence. Rest your fingertips very lightly on either side of the planchette; too much pressure will only make it difficult to move. When the planchette does begin to move, try and sense the nature of any spiritual presence that may be trying to communicate. Do you feel a warm, tingly sensation in your fingertips? Is it cold and unsavory? Ask immediately if the spirit or presence is of the Light—that is, a good or benevolent being. If the answer is no, immediately remove your fingers from the planchette. *Never* try and communicate with a creature of darkness, even in curiosity or fun.

Watch and wait while any message is being spelled out. Write it down or have someone else record it if you can. It is best not to influence the presence with leading questions or repeated ones. Allow the messages to emerge spontaneously for best results, as too much influence or impatience from the querent can influence the nature of your reply. Ask the spiritual presence to identify itself, if you want it to; you may learn more about its life and death. Yet an important factor to take into account in this or any type of spirit communication is that the spirits contacted are those of beings very much like ourselves. They are not above telling you what they think you might like to hear, nor are they necessarily privy to all the available information on the lives of people they do not know. Still it is possible to communicate in many instances and even to make contact with one of your spiritual guides, if you and they are so inclined. If you get strange, nonsensical, or just plain weird messages, try again or switch partners.

Use the messages of the Ouija board if you

can, but never allow them to inordinately influence your decisions, particularly if the advice or predictions you receive stand contrary to that which you already know about yourself and your desires, ambitions, and goals.

Palmistry

Palmistry is a detailed method of divination and character-reading that has come to us from India and the Orient. In the Far East, wise men read not only the hands but also the feet and body of the subject to determine what the future had in store.

It is generally believed that the first palmistry texts were brought to the attention of the ancient Greeks following the conquests of Alexander the Great. We are told that when a prominent palmist read the hands of Aristotle, his students were shocked at the flaws found in his palms. Aristotle, to their amazement, announced the palmist was quite right: The reader had told of the very weak points in his character that he had fought all his life.

Very quickly, palm-reading became a favorite means of divination of the masses. In early Greece and Rome, while women of resource consulted astrologers, those with less material goods visited palmists.

Today, palmistry is one of the few systems in existence that relies on the theory of the *humors*. The theory of the humors was widespread in the Middle Ages, and most medical knowledge and treatments were based on the somewhat primitive theory of physiognomy that determined character, illness, and even treatment based on physical type. It is an interesting cultural amalgam: Almost every culture in the world has contributed in one way or another to palmistry theory.

The first thing to consider when reading a person's palm is the shape of the hand and the relationship of the fingers to the size of the palm. Most people have a combination of hand shapes, so it will be rare to find a "pure" shape in the varieties presented by your friends and subjects.

It was popular in the sixteenth and seventeenth centuries to identify hand shapes and humors according to the elements. A water hand was thought to be phelgmatic, while the air hand indicated a sanguine personality. Choleric people had fire hands, and the earth hand indicated a melancholic disposition. Water and air hands were classified as feminine. Earth and fire were deemed masculine.

The Earth Hand

If you have chunky square palms and your longest finger is a little shorter than the length of the palm, you probably have an earth hand. Earth hands tend to be fleshy, with few lines. The lines will probably be deep. Earth people are intensely physical, and they change the environment around them through physical means. They are straightforward and honest, blunt and passionate. A negative earth hand indicates a violent nature.

The Air Hand

This hand is strongly built. The palm is usually square and the fingers long. An air hand belongs to a person who lives by his or her mind, a person who prefers thought to action. There may be many finely drawn lines on the palm. Rapid communication of thoughts, impulses, and ideas is essential to people with air hands. They may be worriers, but they will undoubtedly be creative.

The Fire Hand

Fire people have palms that are longer than they are wide. The fingers will be noticeably shorter than the length of the palm, and the lines, unlike the lines of the air hand, will be deeply etched, though just as numerous. Fire people are intuitive and strong. They do, however, have a tendency to blow hot and cold. Whatever mode you find them in, they are convincing to those around them and find it easy to get the support of others. Fire people are extroverts and may find themselves in the public eye, or at least notorious among their circle of friends.

The Water Hand

People who have long, thin hands and long, thin fingers are deeply sensitive. Often possessing pronounced psychic ability, they are greatly influenced by their surroundings. Their palms are usually covered with a mesh of thin, fine lines. Negatively, these people have trouble making decisions and may have a tendency to develop neurotic disorders if their energies are not channeled into constructive areas.

Other hand shapes and their significances are as follows.

The Square Hand

Square-handed people have logical, methodical personalities. These are individuals who have enormous tenacity in the face of difficulties or obstacles. They are faithful and dependable and may tend to lack imagination.

The Spatulate Hand

A crooked, knotty hand with flattened, spade-like fingers denotes a person with oceans of energy at his or her disposal. Erratic in their emotional life, they prefer to weather the storm with the help of an oddball sense of humor.

The Conic Hand

Conics have hands that are flexible and medium sized. Their thumbs are small and their fingertips cone shaped. Often artists, at the very least conic personalities are attracted to beauty and art. Large-thumbed conics are obsessed by fame and the comfort that wealth can supply. If the palm is fleshy, the evident love of beauty may be channeled into sensualism. Conics are highly imaginative and will often choose to live in elaborately constructed worlds of their own making, insulated against the more sordid realities of life.

The Philosophic Hand

Large, awkward-looking hands with prominent veins and knobby knuckles indicate a born intellectual and problem-solver, a person who will ferret out the truth as though his or her life depended upon it. These individuals believe in freedom above all. Ethics and justice are important to them; they are fair-minded and often choose a moderate life-style.

Once the shape of the hand has been established, the palm-reader then takes into account the importance of the arrangement of the fleshy pads on the palms. Called the mounts, these are found at the base of the thumb and at the base of each finger. The long pad along the outside of the palm opposite the thumb in called the Mount of the Moon.

If a person's mounts are firm and fleshy, he or she is sensual and sexy. If the mounts are lightly padded or nonexistent, you have probably encountered a dreamer, particularly if the Mount of the Moon is well developed.

The meanings of the mounts are as follows.

Mount of Venus

Located underneath the thumb, a well-developed Mount of Venus speaks of empathy and sensitivity to the needs of others. Love and being loved in return is of utmost importance, as is seeing the beauty in the world at large. However, a person with a well-developed Mount of Venus and a marked Mount of the Moon will become despondent if forced to live in an ugly or discordant environment.

Mount of Mars

This is the small pad between the thumb and index finger. If prominent, it indicates a courageous person who will fight for the rights of others. If overdeveloped, it speaks of an aggressive personality who will pick a fight with little or no prompting.

Mount of Jupiter

This mount is found under the index finger. If it is well developed, the individual will have no problem making money or achieving success—his or her way. Often these people enjoy leading others and find themselves in the corporate or judicial spotlight. But if this mount is excessively prominent in relation to the hand as a whole, the person will delight in riding roughshod over the wishes of others.

Mount of Saturn

To the left of the Mount of Jupiter, this mount indicates the individual is interested in scholarly or philosophic matters. They may also have a religious or occult bent. If underdeveloped, there is reason to believe the person is moody, depressive, and anti-social.

Mount of the Sun

Moving to the left of the Mount of Saturn, the reader will find the Mount of the Sun. Development in this area indicates an artistic person gifted in one or more of the humanities. If overdeveloped, it suggests a dramatic, self-involved ego who wants to be the star of the show. Otherwise, it indicates a social, witty person.

Mount of Mercury

Placed under the little finger, this mount designates a stimulating, often highly verbal and lucky personality who is charming and fun. If overdeveloped, the tendency is to become scattered, restless, and easily bored with routine and mundane matters of daily life.

Mount of Mars

Located directly under the Mount of Mercury, the Mount of Mars, like its opposite mount located between the thumb and index finger, designates a fighter. But on the outside of the hand, the Mount of Mars indicates a person who will rarely fight for the interests of others, preferring his or her own.

Mount of the Moon

This mount is found on the lower outside edge of the hand, on the side of the little finger. If it is developed it indicates a romantic and idealistic person; if overdeveloped, look for a person who can spend hours brooding or using mood-altering substances; the worst case is a person who has difficulty telling fantasy from reality.

Always remember that when reading palms, the entire hand must be taken into consideration. Negative aspects are often balanced by positive aspects in other areas of the hand. If negative aspects are augmented, you may be faced with a worst-case scenario. This is, thankfully, extremely rare. It is also important to remember that the lines in the hand change rapidly. In a matter of weeks, crosses can turn into squares, and lines can lengthen, shorten, or intersect depending upon the attitude of the subject. Palm-reading points out tendencies and characteristics that influence the future.

Once the shape of the hand and the mounts have been studied, the lines of the hand are examined. A quick glance at your palms will reveal that the lines on the right palm and the left palm rarely match. If you are right-handed, read the right hand; the reverse is done if you are left-handed. Traditional beliefs state that the hand that is unused is what you have brought into the world with you, while the hand that is often used indicates what you have done with all this raw material.

Meanings of the Lines

The Life Line

The life line curves around the thumb. Traditionally, the longer the life line, the longer a person's life. But modern palmists often avoid definitive statements to this effect, believing that a person's mental attitude has a great deal to do with the length of his or her life. It is more usual to read the life line as an indication of vitality. Breaks in the line may indicate illness or accident-prone periods.

If the life line begins at the head line (the line running horizontally across the palm), the person is strongly influenced by mental suggestion and would respond well to hypnosis or autosuggestion in bettering his or her life. This marking also indicates a shrewd, businesslike approach to problems. Negatively, it's an individual whose emotions are ruled by intellect.

A life line beginning on the Mount of Jupiter denotes an ambitious person born to rule. If the life line begins below the head line, the person is impulsive and finds the practical considerations of life troublesome.

The Head Line

The head line runs across the middle of the palm from beneath the Mount of Jupiter to the Mount of the Moon. If it begins on the Mount of Mars, or if there are lines sloping from the head line to this mount, the person has difficulty on deciding upon a course of action and sticking with it. If other elements in the hand correspond, watch out. You are dealing with a born fighter who likes to fight for the sake of fighting.

If the head line begins at the Mount of Jupiter, you are facing a multitalented leader, a good manager who will nevertheless manage to get his or her way due to a combination of great good humor and limitless energy. If the head line runs straight across the palm with no breaks, the person is straight thinking and practical, with a good deal of working common sense, comforted by practical friends and possessions that give him or her a feeling of security. A line that begins straight and slopes down indicates a person in which the qualities of imagination and practicality are well balanced. If the line slopes sharply and branches or ends on the Mount of the Moon, the individual is highly imaginative and may have an eccentric life-style, with lots of friends involved in the experimental arts.

Branches from the head line to the various mounts may be read as follows:

- To the Mount of Jupiter: The mind will be used to achieve power and ambition.
- To the Mount of Saturn: Mental occu-

pation with scientific or religious problems.
- To the Mount of the Sun: A person who seeks fame.
- To the Mount of Mercury: The mind will excel in business and profit from travel.

The Heart Line

This is the line found above the head line, below the fingers. In some hands an additional line may be found directly below the fingers. This is not the heart line; it is the Girdle of Venus.

Idealistic, romantic lovers possess heart lines beginning on the Mount of Jupiter. If not greatly threatened by the harsh realities of marriage, this can indicate a person who happily gives his or her heart once and for all. Should the loved one lapse into the frailties of a flesh-and-blood human being, however, this is a person who will hold a grudge forever and hate as heartily as he or she once loved.

People whose heart line begins between the index and second finger have a common-sense approach to love. They have lusty physical appetites as a general rule, though they may not marry for love unless it is to their ultimate material advantage or the spouse has excellent prospects.

If a heart line begins at the mount of Saturn, the person has strong sexual appetites that must be satisfied at all costs. The feeling of the other party can, unfortunately, fall by the wayside.

If the heart line branches toward the head or life lines, the emotions are held in balance by mental faculties. At best, these people are platonic lovers; at worst, they are cold fish. If the heart line is quite curved, the person has a great desire to love and be loved in return. If straight across the palm, emotions are not important in the person's life. If there is no heart line at all, this is not a person to be trusted and is one who will control others at any cost.

The Fate Line

The fate line runs vertically from the wrist to the fingers. Sometimes it is absent or partial; other times it is doubled. A double line indicates success in more than one career. If a fate line begins at the life line, the person will have the support of others, although the person may have a hard time breaking free from their early background and may have to wait until the second half of his or her life to achieve success. A line beginning at the wrist and running to the Mount of Saturn indicates sure success; if it runs above the mount, the person can be a workaholic. Lines beginning at the Mount of the Moon show the person who will achieve success through imagination or public notoriety. Fate lines with forks show that success will be supplemented with the help of many other people. Branches toward the Mount of Jupiter indicate early success; those toward the sun mean that success comes later on; branches toward Mercury indicate success in the field of communications and travel.

If the line stops on the heart line, it indicates success marred by sexual misadventures or irregular liaisons. If it stops at the head line, the person would be well advised to develop better judgment. If the fate line is broken, chained, or otherwise poorly marked, it indicates someone whose life is marked by vicissitudes; but life, nevertheless, will certainly be exciting. Fate lines that begin in the middle of the palm and branch toward the Mount of Mars show that rough beginnings will be overcome by determination and grit. A person whose fate line is forked at the base will be torn between the practical and the mystical throughout his or her lifetime.

The Girdle of Venus

If the Girdle of Venus appears on the palm, it indicates a person who is moody and must fight manic-depressive tendencies. Conversely, it gives the bearer empathetic and sensitive attunement to the needs of others. The Girdle of Venus appears under the middle two fingers above the line of the heart.

Line of the Sun

This line runs vertically across the palm in the general parallel direction of the fate line. If both lines are strongly marked, it indicates great success, particularly in the arts. If one or the other is faint or broken, the fate line and line of the sun will augment each other and avert any tendency to tragedy. If the line of the Sun is absent in an otherwise artistic hand, it means the person will realize recognition for his or her achievements only after he or she is dead.

Line of Health

Oddly enough, the best line of health is no line at all. Although dire predictions surrounded it in the past, its appearance on the palm is a sign the person should take more than average care of his or her health. The line of health runs diagonally across the palm from the fate line toward the Mount of Mercury.

Line of Mars

The line of Mars can be found curved inside the life line on the Mount of Venus. It bestows great energy and vitality upon the owner and indicates courage and bravery in the face of adversity. However, when things are going well, the person may tend toward argumentative and even quarrelsome behavior.

Line of Intuition

Most frequently found on women's palms, this line indicates a highly sensitive nature that is strongly psychic. It curves from the Mount of the Moon to the Mount of Mercury.

Line of Marriage

Traditionally, the horizontal lines across the Mount of Mercury indicate marriages. Now

they are more often read as key relationships with the opposite sex. The most satisfactory line of marriage runs parallel to the
heart line, and the closer it is to the heart
line, the earlier the marriage. Drooping lines
indicate the death of a mate, while forked
lines or crosses, mean divorce. A line that
curves sharply upward indicates the person
may very well never form any satisfactory
alliances. Marriage lines running closely
parallel to each other indicate an extramar-
ital affair.

Unusual Markings

In addition to the shape of the hands, the
lines, and the mounts, there are certain
markings upon the mounts that have special meaning.

The Star

A star is a formation of from five to eight
rayed lines that appear anywhere on the
palm. When apocalyptic hand-reading was
in vogue, stars were interpreted as horren-
dous tragedy. Today, stars are extremely
fortunate signs. If a star appears:

On the Mount of Jupiter: Toward the index finger, the person will achieve fame in his or her own right, especially if the fate, head, and sun lines are strong. If the star appears further down on the mount, the person will associate with the rich, famous, and powerful but will be unable to attain these qualities individually.

On the Mount of Saturn: If the star appears on the line of the sun, the arts will bring the individual great fortune and success. If the star stands alone and is centered on the mount, he or she will have tremendous financial success in the arts. If the star occurs off-mount near the finger or heart line, the person will have wide association with the art world but may not achieve lasting fame.

On the Mount of Mercury: A perfectly centered star on this mount indicates brilliance in one's chosen field. This will most likely be in the areas of finance or theoretical science.

On the Mount of Mars: Between the thumb and index finger, the star marks a person who has great potential for military success or, alternatively, in metalwork or union organization. A star on the Mount of Mars on the other side of the hand indicates that success will be assured through endurance, long suffering, patience, and guts.

On the Mount of Venus: Success and brilliance will come from romantic alliances and passionate relationships. If low on the mount, the person will be surrounded by others who have found success through love and passion, but the individual may not be able to achieve this personally.

The Cross

Whereas stars denote great success and happiness, the cross foretells hardship, trouble, and obstacles that cannot be overcome. At their worst, they indicate lost hope and disillusionment. Remember to read the rest of the hand to find the balancing forces at work affecting this sign.

On the Mount of Jupiter: The only favorable placement for a cross, here it is read as great and lasting affection at some point in the person's life. This is an influence that will bring nothing but good.

On the Mount of Saturn: A gloomy, depressed person who has a tendency to withdraw from all social interaction.

On the Mount of Mercury: Risky business ventures and shaky financial ground. Conversely, someone who devotes his or her life to success in the sciences, which is never realized.

On the Mount of the Sun: A patron of the arts who perceives him- or herself as an artist. Or a person who achieves notoriety through foolish associations.

On the Mount of Venus: Inappropriate lovers or quarrelsome relationships with the opposite sex.

On the Mount of the Moon: An overly imaginative and deceptive personality. A born liar.

On the Fingertips: A person determined to interfere in the lives of others or one who takes on new ventures and never sees anything through.

The Square

Naturally, it is impossible to live life without obstacle or difficulty. But difficulty can be turned to good advantage. The square is the sign of danger averted, of obstacles overcome and used to the best advantage in the situation at hand. We include these meanings for the positioning of the square:

On the Mount of Jupiter: Overambitious ideals will be overcome.

On the Mount of Saturn: Danger associated with isolationist, antisocial behavior will be overcome.

On the Mount of the Sun: Averting of danger associated with lust for fame.

On the Mount of Mercury: Danger due to restlessness or obsession with scientific learning overcome.

On the Mount of Venus: Overcoming danger due to inappropriate affection.

On the Mount of the Moon: Danger associated with a sick or overactive imagination is overcome.

On the Life Line: Mortal danger averted.

On the Head Line: Insanity averted.

On the Heart Line: Last-minute aversion of emotional problems or danger in a primary relationship.

On the Fate Line: Through no fault of the person's own, obstruction in his or her fate by others, either intentionally or through their ignorance. Not only is this overcome, but it works as a positive force in the person's life.

Circles and Spots

Circles and spots are traditionally read as ill omens, although most modern palmists do not attach great importance to this. Circles mean lack of success on the mount on which they appear. The one exception is a circle on the Mount of the Sun, which means outstanding success in the arts. Islands show illness or loss, depending upon which lines or mounts they occur.

Grills

There are few people in the world who do not possess one or more grill formations somewhere on the palm. Grills are tendencies to be watched closely. They can be read as follows:

On the Mount of Jupiter: Egotistical, self-aggrandizing, overly ambitious tendencies.

On the Mount of Saturn: A solitary and gloomy personality.

On the Mount of the Sun: May be vain, frivolous, and shallow.

On the Mount of Mercury: A person who can become unstable in all his or her ways.

On the Mount of the Moon: Someone driven to dominate others at all cost.

On the Mount of Venus: Fickle affections; someone who has a tendency to bounce from one relationship to another.

Triangles, Arrowheads, and Tripods

A triangle tells of a happy future when found anywhere on the hand. Although not as brilliantly successful as the star, a triangle speaks of surefootedness acquired through craft, knowledge, and experience. It is success well earned. A tripod or arrowhead enhances the meaning of the triangle.

On the Mount of Jupiter: An organization person par excellence, with great talent for running large organizations or groups of people.

On the Mount of the Sun: Exceptional ability in the visual arts with the attitude of modesty and humility accompanying great success.

On the Mount of Saturn: Exceptional ability in the occult or religion and the know-how to present this knowledge understandably to the masses.

On the Mount of Mercury: Success in business, speculation, and travel, or, alternatively, a person who is much in the public eye through the mass media.

On the Mount of Mars: An excellent strategist with a cool head and untold resources of courage and clearheadedness in the face of danger and adversity.

On the Mount of the Moon: Well-managed imagination and intuition. Someone who can create believable fantasy worlds. Often a writer engaged in sci-fi or fantasy literature.

On the Mount of Venus: A happy and thoroughly satisfying emotional life.

Mystic Cross

This is a cross found in the center of the hand between the head and heart lines. If it branches toward or forms part of the fate line, the person's life will in some way be connected with religious expression or mystical experience.

How to Read the Palm

There are many different ways to read the palm. Using these guidelines for interpreting the marks on the hand as a foundation, let your intuition guide you in your final reading. It is a good idea to read a person's palms in broad daylight when the nuances of the lines are fully defined. Early hours and north light are best. Reading undertaken by lamp or candlelight in a darkened room are not as effective, although the atmosphere may lend mystery and mood to the reading.

It is interesting to observe how quickly the lines on the palm change. For this reason, some people like to keep a record of palms. One good way to do this is to cover the entire surface of the palm, including the fingers, with ink. Press the palm down on the surface of a clean white sheet of paper and record the name of the person and the date. Make palm prints of both the right and left hands. If you repeat this procedure in three weeks, you will be surprised at how many lines on the palm have changed.

Perhaps the most effective way of recording palm prints is to simply photocopy the palms of the hands. This will reveal the lines and configurations even more accurately than the ink process. The intensity of the palm print can be adjusted and enlarged for specific areas of consideration.

Pendulums

The types and styles of divinatory pendulums are as varied as the people who use them, and the method itself has always been popular, as it is easy, accessible, and inexpensive, even for the novice. In nineteenth-century America, for example, pendulums were widely used to discern the sex of unborn children. The mother lay on her back, and the diviner held the pendulum three inches above her belly, concentrating on the child within. Soon the pendulum began to move. If it swung around in a circle, the child was a girl; if it moved up and down in a more or less vertical line, the child was a boy.

Divinatory pendulums can be constructed of anything. A needle and thread, a small stone, a button or coin, a favorite piece of jewelry, a crystal, or a small sachet stuffed with herbs used in divination—

patchouli, mugwort, and bay leaves—are all excellent choices.

To construct a pendulum, simply secure an object to a string or thread six to ten inches long or the length of your hand measured from the wrist to the tip of the middle finger. There are those who insist that silk is the best choice for a pendulum cord, but any natural fiber or thread will do nicely. Tie the cord to the pendulum, taking care that it swings freely and is well balanced. The weight of the object is a matter of preference; some prefer a pendulum with some weight to insure that the answers obtained will not simply be the result of drafts; others prefer the lightest pendulum possible—a needle or a pin—for best results. Use your own judgment.

The Methods

In divinatory tradition, no other equipment is really necessary to use a pendulum. In its simplest, yes-or-no form, take the pendulum in your left hand, concentrate upon your question, and allow it to fall until it dangles freely above any surface. Hold it very still, and before long the pendulum will begin to move in answer to your inquiry. If it moves in a circle, the answer to your question is yes; if it moves in a line, back and forth, the answer is no. If it doesn't move at all, the answer to your question is unknown, or you are inquiring something about which you are not meant to know at this time.

A small elaboration of the above method is to draw a circle, nine inches in diameter. Write the word *yes* at the top and bottom of the circle, *no* at either side. Proceed and interpret your answer based on where the pendulum moves.

A still more complex method that will provide you with other than yes-and-no answers is to draw a larger circle on a piece of paper or board and divide it evenly into twenty-six segments, labeling each segment with a letter of the alphabet. Hold your pendulum above the center of the circle and concentrate upon the question at hand. With time and patience, the pendulum will swing, spelling out your answer.

Finally, here is a method for the romantically inclined: If you are having trouble choosing between lovers, mark their names on a circle as above. Hold the pendulum centered above the circle and concentrate on the possibilities and qualities of each. The pendulum will begin to swing, and you will know whom to choose.

Rings

A variant that is considerably more complicated than divination by pendulum, divination by rings, or *dactyloscopy*, dates back to ancient Egypt or, some believe, to the mysterious lost continent of Atlantis. In the original practice, small rings were fashioned from seven sacred planetary metals, set with a corresponding precious stone, and engraved with a symbol sacred to the god or goddess of each planet, as follows:

The ring of the *Sun* was made of gold, set with diamond or chrysalite, and engraved with the head of the lion.

The ring of *Saturn* was made of lead, set with garnet, and pictured a coiled serpent.

The ring of *Venus* was made of copper, set with an emerald, and stamped with the sign of the lovers.

The ring of *Mercury* was made of tin or,

preferably, solid quicksilver, set with a cornelian, and showed wings.

The ring of *Mars* was made of iron, set with ruby, and engraved with a sword.

The ring of *Jupiter* was made of tin or platinum, set with topaz, and pictured an eagle.

The ring of the *Moon* was made of silver, set with crystal, and engraved with a crescent sign.

Unless you happen to be a jeweler or metalsmith, or wealthy enough to simply specially order the above, divination by rings may be impractical for you. But if you do choose to pursue the art, very acceptable and less expensive rings can be fashioned in the metals listed above out of wire. Coil perhaps two inches of each type of metal wire around a form or your own finger three times; cut any extra ends and proceed. Store each wire ring separately with an appropriate label, as a tin ring and one made of solid quicksilver can be easily confused on sight.

The Method

The ring used is determined by the day of the consultation. The days of the week and their planetary rulers are listed below:

Day	Ruler	Metal
Saturday	Saturn	Lead
Sunday	Sun	Gold
Monday	Moon	Silver
Tuesday	Mars	Iron
Wednesday	Mercury	Tin or quicksilver
Thursday	Jupiter	Tin or platinum
Friday	Venus	Copper

Three sets of twenty-six small slips of paper or discs, each inscribed with a letter of the alphabet, are then shuffled and spread, face up, on a table. The appropriate ring is then attached to a linen, cotton, or silk thread and allowed to hang suspended over the letters, while the diviner and the querent concentrate on the issue at hand. Mentally invoke the help of the day's planetary god and burn the thread. The ring will fall and roll around the table. Note every letter over which it passes and write each down. Repeat this action six more times for a total of seven. The reply to the question is then formed from the letters—which must be unscrambled. Any leftover letters are taken to be initials for the words of a clarifying sentence that will, with meditation, be subsequently revealed to you.

Runes

Runes are an oracle derived from the alphabet of northern European peoples. The last rune masters lived in seventeenth-century Iceland, and, because their wisdom was passed down by oral tradition from spiritual warrior to spiritual warrior, much of this wisdom has faded with time. Add to that the disfavor incurred by Hitler, who used a double rune, SIG, to identify his stormtroopers, and you will perhaps understand why it has only been in the last fifteen years or so that runes have experienced a reemergence in the divinatory arts. Incidentally, SIG means "victory."

Originally, runes were used to ward off evil and to cast spells as well as an oracle. Although many of the stories and sagas of the Germans, Vikings, and Celts were subsequently recorded from the original oral traditions, much of the magic and lore of rune-reading has been lost. Those with an affinity for rune-reading will know it almost immediately. The symbols will seem strangely recognizable, and the world that they speak of will be astonishingly comfortable and familiar.

Because runes are an oracle, they will not give you a yes or no answer that is easy to grasp and understand. The runes will describe a situation and suggest ways of acting to enable the querent to navigate his or her way through a given problem; do not expect them to solve a problem for you. Runes concern themselves with the soul's journey—an awareness of the True Self that leads to enlightenment.

Casting the runes requires a thoughtful, unhurried attitude but perhaps not as intellectual a bent of mind as the I Ching. The runes are active messengers, and their readings can often be quite cataclysmic. Patience and familiarity with the symbols will help the reader to derive satisfactory readings from these intriguing and fascinating symbols that speak of ice, snow, frost, and violent spring thaws.

The rune alphabet consists of twenty-four symbols and a single blank rune. You may buy commercial runes or make your own. If you choose to make your own, be as inventive as you like. You can collect small, smooth stones you find by the water and paint the letters on their surface, or you can cut small pieces of wood, sand them down, and carve the rune letters into their surface. If you are in a hurry, take a piece of poster-board and cut it into twenty-four uniform squares, with an additional square for the blank rune. Use a magic marker or thick pen and record one letter on each square. When not in use, it's a good idea to keep your runes in a rune bag—no more than a small sack large enough to hold your runes, usually with a drawstring. If you want a quick consultation, you can rummage around in the bag and pick one out for a quick editorial comment on the problem that is troubling you.

There are two possible interpretations for each rune, depending on whether the rune is drawn upright or reversed. We have included both possibilities in the interpretations that follow.

How to Read Your Runes

One-Rune Method

For a quick answer on any question, con-centrate on the problem at hand, reach into your rune bag, and shuffle the runes with your fingers. Draw out one rune and place it before you. This will describe the situation and recommend a certain course of action or meditation to be followed.

Three-Rune Method

To get a fast and effective reading of the past, present, and future of any situation, concentrate on the problem at hand while shaking the rune bag; reach into the bag and draw out three runes, one rune at a time. Place them in a line from left to right. The first rune drawn represents the past, the center the present, and the future is the one to the right of the spread, or the last rune drawn. Allow yourself some time to look at your runes and their interrelationship to each other. Then refer to the interpretations for insight. The reading is completed when you have placed them all in the bag again. Perhaps more than any method of divination, runes will continue to speak to you the longer you leave them out. Do not be in a hurry, therefore, with your reading.

Celtic Cross

Concentrate on the problem you wish to address. Shake the rune bag and draw out six runes. Place the first rune down. The second rune is placed to the right, the third to the left, the fourth at the bottom of the cross, the fifth at the top, and the sixth directly above the fifth.

The runes are to be read in this order:

1: The self.
2: The past.
3: The future.
4: The fundamental issue at hand.
5: The obstacle that has come between you and the achievement of your goal.
6: The best outcome you can anticipate, based on the current situation.

The Rune Symbols

MAN This is the rune of self. It is first a reminder—"To thine ownself be true"—and second a gentle caution. The past is continually passing, says this rune, and the future is always ahead of you. Concentrate on those things that are truly important—that which abides. It is not a time to seek glory but to concentrate on your work for its own sake.

Reversed: Look within for that which is blocking your progress. Do not blame others but admit that that which impedes you comes from within. Release it, and all will be well.

GIFU This is the rune of partnership. A union or joining together of some kind is imminent. Remember that true partnership, love, or conjoining can be achieved only when the parties involved each retain their wholeness and separate natures. It is the rune that signifies a gift. The adage "If you love someone, let them go" applies here, for the gift of liberation is the state from which all others originate. It has no reverse.

OSS This is the messenger rune, signifying news, communications, and portents. Pay special attention to meetings, new people, and casual encounters now: They might be trying to tell you something. It is a time to delve beyond the surface in an attempt to integrate your conscious and subconscious.

Reversed: Misunderstandings, failed communications, and misdirected conversations are all apparent now. You may feel you have been led on a wild goose chase, yet the message here is clear: Adversity is a great teacher.

ⷪ ᴏᴅᴀʟ This is the rune of acquisition and benefits. Yet whatever you receive now may involve some sacrifice on your part. You may feel that the time has come to separate from your background and close associates or from an old way of thinking. It is part of your path. Submit to forces larger than yourself, and retreat when you know the time is right.

Reversed: Do not be caught up in tradition or feel that you can wend your way through a situation while flying on "automatic pilot." Honesty is of the essence now; refusing to see the value in separation or departures may result in pain for others. It is not, however, a time for action. Wait for the universe to move, then follow as you know you must.

ᚢ ᴜʀ A rune that reflects endings and beginnings. Your habits may have become outmoded, yet you must pass through a period of darkness before you can reemerge into the light of growth and change. See your losses now as opportunities, and adapt yourself to the demands of a creative time. In emotional matters, this rune signifies that you may have to let go of someone to whom you have a deep attachment—someone through whom, in fact, you have been living in some way. You must now reclaim that aspect for your own and live it to its fullest. Since a change within the self is never by force, remember that the new is always more powerful than the old.

Reversed: Minor setbacks should serve to put you on notice that greater change is called for. If you find yourself in over your head, start swimming.

ᚲ
PEORTH   This is a mystery rune that indicates hidden forces are at work in your situation. The externals don't matter now—what is important will show itself in time. There is a transformation at work within you now; your inner integrity is seeking its own level, and renewal is sure to follow.

Reversed: Don't expect too much now. Concentrate on yourself and be careful not to repeat patterns you have outgrown. Above all, negativity is never lasting. Keep your sense of humor.

ᚾ
NAWT   This is a complicated and difficult rune. It tells of restrictions and necessities, limitations and pain. Probe the dark areas of your life, the places where your weaknesses dwell, and do not project them onto others. Pain is now to be examined—what

draws misfortune to you? In another sense, this rune's message is simple: Restore balance, and progress will follow.

Reversed: In the greatest darkness there will appear a light, if only a pinpoint. When something in your life has been cast out, it causes disruption. Keep your faith and persevere.

ING This symbol speaks of the need to be desired, the yearning to share. In personal matters, you need to harmonize with others. Complete projects, and clear away what is insignificant. In order for a garden to grow, the ground must be prepared. This is a rune of fertility: New beginnings are in the offing, yet remember that movement always involves risk. Wait for improvement with confidence and calm. There is no reverse.

YR You cannot make your influence felt now. Do not be in a rush to proceed with or to resolve matters. Be patient, and exercise foresight by being aware that every action has a consequence. There is always a period of waiting before a harvest. There is no reverse.

AKZI Control your emotions. There is plenty of activity around you now, and highs as well as lows beckon from all quarters. Do not undertake challenge for its own sake: weigh possible unwanted influences against possible rewards. Timing and correctness are ultimate—knowing that is the best protection against difficulty.

Reversed: Be aware of your health and avoid excess. Know that you may undertake to form associations with people who are using you, and retain your identity and purpose. You may lose the battle but never the war, as long as your self-awareness is in place.

A fortunate rune. Your ambitions will be realized, love fulfilled, rewards received. Yet reward must be examined: Do you seek it for its own sake or because such rewards enable you to truly take charge of your destiny? Be vigilant and do not be reckless. Use your good fortune to better the lives of others, for we are all one.

Reversed: This is the sign of a multitude of frustrations, and your rewards, if you receive them at all, will almost certainly be dubious. Ask yourself: What can this teach me?

The rune of joy and enlightenment. This is the place where knowledge and experience merge into understanding. You will experience a clarification, a flash of insight, after which circumstances will fall into place. Rejoice.

Reversed: Some kind of crisis is at hand—things are taking too long not to cause concern, or you may find your enlightenment is being clouded by fixed beliefs and outworn tradition. This rune can indicate that you must center yourself, away from your anxiety, before you can be open to enlightenment. Perhaps you should draw again, after you've calmed down.

YER There will be a beneficial resolution to your situation but only after a period of time has elapsed and the current cycle is completed. This rune advises patience and perseverance, careful nurturing of a situation, without necessarily being assured that its outcome will be what you had in mind. Don't push. There is no reverse.

KAON The darkness will give way to the light, just as the sunrise illuminates the sky by degrees. This is not the flash of insight indicated elsewhere but the gradual dispelling of confusions and *un*-awareness. In relationships, this may be a time of improved understanding, a gradual letting down of defenses, and greater intimacy, yet it will be your responsibility to set the new phase in motion.

Reversed: You must recognize now that the old is passing away. There will be loss, but then again there is little point in clinging to that which is already gone. See the opportunity in this: When one door closes, another opens.

↑

TIW This rune states that it is time to act as you will, yet at the same time be willing to take the consequences of your actions and recognize that no outcome is ever assured. Be the warrior who fights out of conviction, and let that be all the cause you need. Travel lightly, without that which is extraneous, and do not fight foolishly or without restraint. If your cause is just, if your beliefs are true, the war is won. If this rune appears in regard to a love relationship, it indicates that this person is a soul mate. You have things to accomplish together.

Reversed: Examine your motives. Do not attempt to dominate a person or situation just because you can. Do not be caught up in results or activities for their own sakes. Time your battles carefully and choose them well.

B

BIRCA Fertility leads to growth. Your plans will come to flower with modesty, patience, and perseverance. Through gentleness, you can affect outcomes now. Cleanse your motives and examine your intentions. Delve deeply.

Reversed: You may feel that you have missed a chance or failed to take an opportunity. Recognize that obstacles to growth always exist within the self—once identified, they can be vanquished.

M
EOH   The rune of movement or progress, this can indicate relocation, new environments, and changes for the better. It is a gradual development at work here, rather than a sudden change, the firm foundation on which new structures can be built. You have made progress, but do not lapse into complacency. Look to your future with confidence and proceed as you must.

Reversed: Opportunity may be knocking now, but recognize that you may not be the one who's supposed to answer the door. Watch your timing and do not undertake projects or busy work for their own sake. The need to do something may be strong now, but be assured that you are certain to get what's coming to you.

↑
LAGU   Immerse yourself in the flow—experience without needing to understand and

approach everything with the innocence and enthusiasm of a child. This rune may signal the opening up of psychic powers: It is a lunar rune, and it speaks to the feminine, more receptive side of our natures. Study and prepare; attune yourself to the tides of nature. When drawn with regard to romantic attachments, it speaks of happy endings—a sacred union—that which was meant to be.

Reversed: If you feel unbalanced or unfulfilled, it is because you are not in touch with or ignoring your instincts and inner voice. Get busy.

ᚺ HAGAL   Your need for growth may be at the center of the cataclysms in your life. In some cases, destruction, breaking free, and a complete letting go may be what is necessary before you can truly be what you are. Things are almost certainly going awry for you, but remember that these are not external forces so much as they are a reflection of your internal needs and desires. There is no reversed reading for this rune.

ᚱ RIT   Remember that you were never intended to be entirely self-reliant. Seek the help and advice of others if the situation seems to call for it. On another level, you are striving for union—with your inner and outer beings, with another, with the universal mind. Rest assured that obstructions will disappear and that matters will come to fruition in their own time. Do not waste yourself in regrets. And prepare, if necessary, to let go of some comforts or material advantages. Seek union with that which you desire.

Reversed: Be particularly attentive to the personal side of your life and relationships with others. There may be arguments, departures, and separations. The important thing now is how you *respond*.

ᚦ
THORN This is the rune of inaction. Recognize that a transformation is at work within you and that you must wait for it to be completed before you can advance into the sphere of successful action. Review your life, your former ambitions, and the person who is passing away. Make no decisions.

Reversed: A rite of passage can be easy or difficult; the quality of the experience is largely up to the individual. Self-pity is never appropriate. There are those who contemplate out of choice, while others have a period of contemplation thrust upon them. Do not let an awareness of your failings drive you to unfortunate or hasty choices.

ᛞ
DAG The times call for unquestioning faith. You may be experiencing a transfor-

mation in your life; welcome it. The changes now could be far-reaching and monumental. Sometimes this rune can introduce new prosperity—a new dawn has come; but remember that for any transformation to be successful, work is always required. There is no reverse for this rune.

IS   This is the rune of ice. Symbolizing that which is frozen or suspended, it may give rise to not-unwarranted feelings of doubt and powerlessness. Submit to your circumstances now, knowing that they are not the result of your doing or action but of timing. Do not attempt to cling to what cannot be yours; the ice rune calls for a sacrifice of the ego, for submission, and reflection. Remember that the seeds of spring lie sleeping beneath the ice of winter. There is no reverse .

SIG   This is the rune of wholeness or completion. You must pursue your personal myth—that is the only choice there is. You have great power now, and you may experience regeneration down to the very depths of your being. Know that self-knowledge inevitably results in a course of action—that which we *must* do, even if it means to withdraw from the world. There is profound insight associated with this rune; admit to yourself things you have denied. Be confident without being arrogant, be true without being superior. SIG has no reverse.

The blank rune is that which is unknowable—the beginning and the end, a point of contact with your true destiny. The blank rune can mean death, and it brings our fears to the forefront, yet it should be seen only as another force at work within you—a reminder than you cannot control what is not known and that nothing is predestined.

Sieve Divination

Divination by the sieve is still practiced in areas of Belgium and Brittany, though it was originally found all over France, England, and Scotland. Like the Russian-based divination by keys, *tourner la sas,* or "the turning of the sieve," is primarily used for the purpose of identifying thieves or village wrongdoers. When something is missing or stolen, a sieve is suspended from the rafters by a rope, and the diviner, magician, or village elder invokes the name of God or the patron saint of the village and slowly pronounces the names of the suspects, pausing after each one in order to let the Powers That Be adequately identify the culprit. If the sieve moves or turns after a name is pronounced, the hapless perpetrator (or innocent bystander) is branded a criminal and duly ostracized.

Table-Tipping

Table-tipping is a dramatic form of spirit-rapping wherein the participants seek a communicant from the other side to impart knowledge. The spirit, in theory, infuses its energy into an inanimate object—in this case, a light portable or card table—and combines this energy with that of the seekers to raise and lower the table in response to questions.

The Method

A fairly recent comer to the divinatory arts, table-tipping first appeared in this country as an outgrowth of the spiritualist movement of the late nineteenth century. Table-tipping requires two participants; each sits comfortably on either side of a table (folding card tables are best for the purpose) and places their fingertips lightly on the edge of the table until they both sense a definite presence, usually through a strong, warm, tingling sensation that travels up through the fingertips and into the forearms. Before long, and *without* pushing, the table will tip or rise up and balance on two legs.

Instruct the presence that it is to answer questions thus: one tip or bounce for yes, two for no. Immediately inquire of the spirit present whether or not it is of the Light, and if the answer is no, abandon the table for the moment and try again later when you are certain the presence has departed.

When you have contacted a suitable spirit, you may begin to ask yes and no questions using the format above. Or, if your prefer, you may instruct the spirit to tap out the letters of the alphabet in response to your inquiries, one for A, two for B, and so on. Since receiving messages from beyond in this fashion can get a tad tedious—to say nothing of straining relations with the downstairs neighbors—you may prefer, once you have gotten the method established, to ask the spirit to abbreviate or initial its responses.

Again, *never* attempt to communicate with a spiritual presence that does not stand in the Light or one with whom one or both of the participants feels uncomfortable.

Keep in mind, as with any other form of spiritual contact, that the spirits, while they may indeed be wiser than ourselves, are by no means omniscient. Trust your own inner voice when it comes to following their instructions or advice.

The Tarot

No one is quite certain where the Tarot originated or exactly how long it has been in use. Some scholars attribute the cards to ancient Egypt, others believe they first appeared in the ancient North African city of Fez. Still others insist that the Tarot comes down to us from the lost civilization of Atlantis. In fact, the first deck of Tarot cards that can be documented hails from fifteenth-century Italy, though it seems to be based on a symbolic system that is far older.

And therein lies the key to the Tarot's popular mystique. Of any of the divinatory methods included in these pages, the Tarot perhaps has the most identifiable symbolic system, one that many believe taps into the collective unconscious of humankind and establishes what C. F. Jung called "contact with the archetypes."

The deck itself consists of seventy-eight cards, divided into two parts—the twenty-two cards of the Major Arcana and the fifty-six cards of the Minor Arcana. Traditionally, the cards of the Major Arcana join together to depict the journey of the soul, while the cards of the Minor Arcana consist of four suits that correspond roughly to the playing-card deck and concern themselves with the realms of personal fortune and daily existence. There are many different types and designs of Tarot decks currently on the market, and we suggest you choose one that you find appealing. As a student of the Tarot, it is more than likely that you will find yourself in possession of many different styles of Tarot decks before you are through. For purposes of the novice, we suggest beginning on either the popular Rider Tarot deck or the Waite deck. We recommend these decks for two reasons: First, they are the most readily available in this country, and second, *each* card in these decks bears a pictorial illustration that roughly corresponds to the divinatory significance of the card itself, making learning and reading the cards much easier.

The Methods

A study of all the different types of Tarot spreads could constitute a book in itself. There are the nine-card spread, the Celtic cross, the tree of life, the karmic method, the wish spread, the horoscope method, and the Daath-pack method, just to name a very few. For purposes of introduction, we include here two of the easiest and yet thorough versions, the Celtic cross and the nine-card—or past, present, and future—spread.

The Nine-Card Spread

The querent shuffles the cards from left to right. When you feel that they are sufficiently "warmed up," cut the cards in three piles toward you, three times. Observe the card on the bottom of the deck before laying out the cards. Often it will show you a significant aspect of the situation—the real "question" or subject of the reading. Lay out three cards for the past, three for the present, and three for the future, all in a row, assigning the positions as follows:

1. The distant past.
2. That which is gone but not forgotten.

3. That which is past or passing away, yet bears on the subject, the very recent past.
4. Present influences.
5. Present goals.
6. Present realities.
7. The very near future.
8. That which will influence the subject but is yet to come.
9. The outcome or resolution of the subject or question at hand.

Proceed with the reading, *being careful to interpret the cards in relation to one another.* This cannot be stressed enough. Where the cards fall in relationship to each other can often drastically affect the outcome of a reading. Consider the following example:

The three of swords, generally interpreted as tears, heartbreak, and confusion, whether upright or reversed, falls next to the Page of wands in a reading regarding a young woman's romantic future. Should the three of swords fall in a position of the recent past, *preceding* the Page in the present-influences position, it might indicate that the querent should take advantage of any invitations or social contacts despite recent emotional traumas. If the three of swords falls in the position *following* the Page, the present-goals position of the card becomes secondary to the interpretation—obviously, no one holds tears and confusion as a goal. The woman will meet an attractive person in her very near future, but she is to beware—he will be a real heartbreaker!

The Celtic Cross

The Celtic Cross consists of ten cards or positions, plus a significator. Until you really get to know your deck (and it you), it is a good idea to choose a single significator for every spread you lay out. Simply put, the significator is the face card, generally chosen from the Minor Arcana, that represents you in the deck. Different methods of reading recommend different methods for choosing your significator. You can correspond your card to your astrological sign: A Leo man, for example, would choose the King of wands as his significator, wands being the suit that corresponds to the fire signs of the Zodiac. Cups correspond to water, swords to air, and pentacles or coins to earth. Many interpretive methods describe the face cards in terms of coloring—pentacles people are invariably brunettes with swarthy skin, for example. Still others insist that all young single people are Pages or Knights, while married people, regardless of age, are Kings and Queens. We recommend simply that you separate the face cards of the Minor Arcana from your deck, lay them face up on any surface, meditate on them for a time, and choose one you feel is right—one, in effect, with whom you feel a rapport. Lay your significator—or one for the querent, if it is someone other than yourself—face up on a table, separating it from the others prior to shuffling the deck. After shuffling the cards, spread them out on a table in front of you, face down. Lightly touching the backs of the cards with your fingertips, make twenty-one clockwise circles, concentrating on your question. Now, gather the cards together into a new stack. Place your significator in the center of the table or other flat surface. To complete the Celtic Cross lay the cards out clockwise as follows:

1. Place over the significator: This covers him. It is the most pervasive influence surrounding the querent at the present time.
2. The second card is laid crosswise over the other two. This crosses the querent and represents obstacles that must be overcome.
3. The third card is laid beneath the others. This is below him. This card

represents the foundation of the question—the real issue.

4. The fourth card is laid to the left of the significator. This is the past. It represents an influence that is diminishing.

5. The fifth card is placed above, to form the highest point of the cross. This is above him. It represents the best possible outcome of the present situation.

6. The sixth card is placed to the right. This is before him. It represents a significant future influence.

7. The next cards are placed in a vertical line to the right of the cross. The first card, in the seventh position, is read as the querent's present position.

8. The eighth card, placed above the seventh, speaks of influences that will arise from the querent's position on the question.

9. The ninth card tells of the querent's hopes and fears regarding the situation.

10. The tenth is a key card. It tells of the outcome of the situation—how the question or issue will be resolved.

The Meanings of the Cards

Do keep in mind that the interpretations of the cards as listed below represent only a scratch on the surface, designed only as a quick-reference table. They are by no means comprehensive definitions; we suggest that you refer to the reference manual included with your deck or any of the very many excellent books on the Tarot for further definitions and interpretations to guide you in accurate readings.

The Major Arcana

0. The Fool: A beginning; a choice is offered. *Reversed:* The choice made is likely to be faulty.

1. The Magician: The ability to direct power to your will. Say yes to life. *Reversed:* Indecision, confusion.

2. The High Priestess: Intuition; something hidden or mysterious. Secrets. *Reversed:* Vanity, or reckless sexual passion.

3. The Empress: Creativity, fertility, good fortune. *Reversed:* A negative woman; disputes in relationships.

4. The Emperor: Ambition, aggression,

building. *Reversed:* Blockages to your ambitions; indecision.

5. The Hierophant or High Priest: Tradition, submitting to social norms. Someone to guide you. *Reversed:* Unconventionality, bad advice, disloyalty.

6. The Lovers: A choice in relationships. Attraction, sex. *Reversed:* Sudden loss of relationship; inability to choose.

7. The Chariot: Success despite difficulties, travel, the unexpected. *Reversed:* Bad luck, delays.

8. Justice: A testing period; do not judge others too harshly. *Reversed:* Injustice, things go awry.

9. The Hermit: Withdrawal from the world. Introversion. *Reversed:* Secrecy, the perpetual Peter Pan.

10. Wheel of Fortune: The ups and downs of life. Financial improvements. *Reversed:* A run of bad fortune; unforeseen difficulties.

11. Strength symbolized by a woman and a lion: Inner fortitude. Balancing the material and spiritual. *Reversed:* Lack of courage. Physical passion over spiritual principle.

12. The Hanged Man: A period of suspension in one's life. Surrender to forces beyond your control. *Reversed:* Release, movement. Do not succumb to vain regret.

13. Death: The end of a cycle. Rebirth. Abandonment of the familiar. *Reversed:* New beginnings; dawn follows the dark.

14. Temperance: Wishes will come true. Be modest and wise. Happy outcomes. *Reversed:* Unsuccessful combinations. Excess.

15. The Devil: Sexuality, temptation through the material. *Reversed:* Stupidity, malice. Gossip.

16. The Tower: Conflict, war, and loss, sometimes out of choice or necessity. *Reversed:* Imprisonment through indecision.

17. The Star: Great love, success, and good fortune through spiritual attunement. *Reversed:* Hindrances, reversals. You are not in tune with your inner self.

18. The Moon: The true nature of a situation is obscured or hidden. *Reversed:* Day-to-day hassles and irritations.

19. The Sun: Marriage, happiness, good fortune of all kinds. *Reversed:* Dubious rewards; you will triumph eventually.

20. The Last Judgment: New beginnings, reunions, problems resolved. *Reversed:* Unsatisfactory conclusions or delays.

21. The World: Success on every level. *Reversed:* Boredom, stagnation.

The Minor Arcana

Wands: In general terms, wands govern the areas of new enterprise, adventure, speculation, and activity.

Ace: New beginnings and enterprises. Success through risk. *Reversed:* Unforeseen setbacks; poor planning.

Two: Attainment of needs, boldness, and courage. *Reversed:* Setbacks, loss of faith. Be prepared for the unexpected.

Three: Experience and acumen. Negotiations and commerce. *Reversed:* Ulterior motives, treachery.

Four: Romance and marriage. Prosperity. *Reversed:* Unfulfilled expectations; flawed beauty. Incomplete joy.

Five: Conflict, violent strife. Obstacles and, in some instances, games. *Reversed:* Deception, contradictions. A caution against indecision.

Six: Triumph. Good news is on the way. Obstacles cleared away. *Reversed:* Delays, apprehension, sometimes treachery and malice.

Seven: Meeting challenges successfully. You have the advantage. *Reversed:* Anxiety and embarrassment. Hesitancy and uncertainty.

Eight: Much activity, sudden progress.

Decisions made in haste. *Reversed:* Jealousy, harassment, domestic disharmony.

Nine: Anticipation of trouble. Wait for change. The pause in a struggle. *Reversed:* Obstacles and problems. Adversity. Ill health.

Ten: Many problems or pressures. A sense of being overburdened. The future will be better. *Reversed:* Intrigues and duplicity. Some losses will occur.

Page: An envoy or messenger. Invitations and good news. *Reversed:* A heartbreaker. Instability and gossip.

Knight: Sudden departures or a change of residence. *Reversed:* Ruptures in a relationship. The would-be lover turns disruptive.

Queen: A sympathetic and understanding person. Friendly and magnetic. *Reversed:* Jealousy, deceit, and infidelity.

King: An honest and conscientious man. Devoted, friendly, and educated. *Reversed:* Austerity; an ascetic. Dogmatic and deliberate.

Cups: In general terms, the suit of cups governs the emotions, relationships, and affairs of the heart.

Ace: Ecstasy, great abundance, exquisite joy—but fleeting. *Reversed:* False or unrequited love. Inconstancy and changes for the worse.

Two: Renewed passion and friendship. Partnerships based on emotional understanding; marriage. *Reversed:* Unsatisfactory love. Misunderstanding; lovers at cross-purposes.

Three: Healing and celebration; sexual passion; compromise. *Reversed:* Hedonism, overindulgence, superfluity.

Four: Boredom. Disgust and disappointment; a period of stagnation. *Reversed:* Newness; new contacts, acquaintances, and knowledge.

Five: Flawed or unhappy love. Loss but with something left over. *Reversed:* Hopeful outcomes. New alliances; reunions.

Six: Memories, nostalgia. Longing and an overactive imagination. *Reversed:* The future—opportunities. Unstable plans.

Seven: Fantasy, daydreams, wishful thinking, illusions. *Reversed:* Desire, determination, intelligent choices.

Eight: Things thrown aside as soon as gained. Shyness, modesty. *Reversed:* Renewed effort leads to attainment. Festivity and celebration.

Nine: Success, material attainment; the Wish Card. *Reversed:* The wish will not come true. Excess and disappointment.

Ten: Happiness and contentment. Good family life; great joy. *Reversed:* Loss and betrayal; quarrels and pettiness.

Page: A studious person, one who is helpful and trustworthy. *Reversed:* Inclination, seductions, attraction.

Knight: Advancement and challenge. Invitation or proposition. *Reversed:* Subtlety, deception, and fraud. A swindler.

Queen: A warm-hearted and fair person. Devoted wife and mother; a loving person. *Reversed:* Dishonor and dishonesty.

King: Responsibility and creativity; a learned man. *Reversed:* Double-dealing or injustice. Shifty in business dealings.

Swords: This suit governs the areas of the mind and the intellect, especially reason applied to the problems of daily life.

Ace: Strength, great love and conquest. Fertility. *Reversed:* Blockage, self-destruction, infertility.

Two: Stalemate in affections; military friendships. *Reversed:* Lies, false friends, end to an impasse.

Three: Heartbreak, tears, upheaval, and confusion. Sudden separation. *Reversed:* Error, incompatibility, loss, and alienation.

Four: Rest after extended struggle, solitude, retreat, seclusion. *Reversed:* Renewed activity and guarded advancement; desire to recover what has been lost.

Five: Conquest, destruction of others; enemies will appear. *Reversed:* Uncertainty, weakness, probable chance of defeat.

Six: Journeys; success after anxiety. *Reversed;* No immediate solution to present difficulties. A declaration.

Seven: Persevere through hope and confidence. *Reversed:* Nonsense through uncertain counsel and advice. Ugly rumors.

Eight: Catastrophe, crises, turmoil. *Reversed:* Depression, disquiet, hard work.

Nine: Misery, illness of a loved one, despair, and the pangs of conscience. *Reversed:* Shame, timidity, distrust.

Ten: Complete ruin or affliction, bringing on anguish and feelings of desolation. *Reversed:* A momentary advantage or temporary improvement.

Page: Insight, vigilance, and watchfulness are demanded. Uncovering that which is not obvious. *Reversed:* An imposter and the unforeseen. Be prepared for the unexpected.

Knight: A dashing, heroic young man. Impetuosity. A rush into the unknown. *Reversed:* Impulsive mistakes. Conceit and hubris.

Queen: Intense perception. A subtle person. May mean mourning or loneliness. *Reversed:* Narrowmindedness, ill temper. Desire for vengeance.

King: Authority. A highly analytical person, proficient in his profession. *Reversed:*

Perversity. A person who pursues a matter to ruin.

Coins or Pentacles: Generally speaking, the suit of pentacles governs those areas of life concerned with financial matters, work, gain, and inheritance.

Ace: Attainment, prosperity, riches, ecstasy. *Reversed:* Prosperity without happiness, greed, wasted money.

Two: New projects will have a poor start. Difficulties and worries. *Reversed:* Literary talent, letters, and messages.

Three: Mastery, perfection, renown for one's work, power. *Reversed:* Mediocrity, poor craftmanship, money problems.

Four: Miserliness, inability to share with those in need. Greed. *Reversed:* Loss of material goods, obstacles, suspense, and delay.

Five: Destitution and failure. Impoverishment; lovers who discover one another through similar troubles. *Reversed:* New interests; overcoming domestic disharmony.

Six: Generosity, charity, and kindness. *Reversed:* Selfishness, envy, jealousy; the inability to share oneself.

Seven: Ingenuity, growth, and progress through hard work. *Reversed:* Impatience, uneasiness, and worries. Unwise speculation.

Eight: A quick study. Candor. Personal effort. *Reversed:* Disillusionment, hypocrisy, lack of ambition.

Nine: Prudence, accomplishments, and discretion; material fortune. *Reversed:* Threats, bad faith, possible loss of a valued object or friend.

Ten: Domestic prosperity, security, riches, an inheritance. *Reversed:* Poor odds, hazards, and dissipation.

Page: Introversion, deep concentration, scholarship. *Reversed:* Failure to recognize the obvious, wastefulness, poor logic.

Knight: A dependable person; methodical and persistent. *Reversed:* Carelessness, inertia, lack of direction.

Queen: Opulence, security, generosity, magnificence; a noble soul with a sharp tongue. *Reversed:* Neglected responsibilities, a false sense of security, fear of failure.

King: A person of character and intelligence; a reliable mate and successful business person. *Reversed:* Unfaithfulness; using any means to achieve the end.

Tealeaves

Tealeaf-reading began in the early nineteenth century. Its recent decline is probably due to the invention of the tea bag. As with coffee-ground-reading, it is best when done with plain white cups and a coarse tea blend. Use Indian or British teas, since they have the largest leaves. Chinese teas are fine too. A good formula for making tea is the old standby of a teaspoon of loose tea per person and one for the pot. Leave about a quarter of an inch of tea at the bottom of the cup after drinking it. Swirl the liquid around so the tealeaves are stirred up from the bottom and begin to cling to the sides of the cup, while concentrating on the question at hand. Pour off any extra liquid gently.

Tealeaf-reading requires a fine eye. The leaves do not immediately sort themselves into any recognizable patterns. As recommended with coffee grounds, it is easier if you squint and soften your vision. This makes it easier to discern shapes and symbols in the cup. To determine the timing of coming events, use the following formula: Symbols that appear near the rim of the cup indicate events that will occur near the end of the month; symbols one-third of the way down indicate something that will occur within the next year or eighteen months; those near the bottom of the cup mean something that will take place in two years or more. For a listing of traditional symbol interpretations, refer to the section on coffee grounds. Do remember, however, that such symbols are to be used only as a reference and not as a literal interpretation. Do not hesitate to use your own intuition and insight in readings of this kind. For symbols that don't appear on the list, depend upon your inner voice and feelings for instruction.

Water Divination

Water divination is a form of scrying that is undoubtedly one of the oldest and most practiced in the world. In primitive times, water-scrying was one of the most basic methods of divination, requiring only a still pond or pool and the right attitude, but the art was elaborated on over the years, sometimes in strange and even perverse ways.

Water has always been considered a pure substance and, therefore, reliable in matters of divination. Consider the myths that spirits of the dead and witches, whose souls presumably belong to the underworld, cannot cross large bodies of water, or the practice of binding a witch's hands and feet and throwing her into a nearby river. If the woman sank, she was pure of heart (though understandably drowned), while a witch would float and survive to be burned at the stake.

Seafaring peoples have often used the divinatory arts in an effort to better determine the mysteries of the deep. Coastal peoples of Africa would employ a witch doctor to tie knots in a rope, the numbers of which would calm the seas or raise a storm, depending on the situation. Another tradition, from the British Isles, recommends placing a dish in a milk pan filled with water. If the water is violently agitated by the action, the fate of the fishing boats was sealed: There had been a storm, and the boats were lost. If the water remained calm, all would be well and the boats would return.

One of the more basic divinatory methods that survives from the earlier traditions is as follows: Over a calm pond or a stagnant pool, over which a fair amount of algae has grown, throw three small stones—one round, one triangular, and one cube shaped. The undulations they cause in the water, and the subsequent shapes formed in the scum, are to be interpreted intuitively, much as ink blots, wax-reading, or other forms of scrying.

Wax Divination

Divination by wax, or cereoscopy, comes to us from Greece by way of England. The process requires very fine wax, such as beeswax or paraffin, which is melted in a brass bowl over very low heat and stirred gently with a spatula until it is entirely liquified. It is of the greatest importance that this be done over very low heat, in a double boiler or in a pan filled with water. Any form of wax easily ignites should it get too hot or be directly exposed to flame.

The Method

With the question fixed in the querent's mind, the wax should be poured slowly into another brass bowl filled with ice-cold water. The wax will spread in thin layers, and within minutes, discernible shapes will form from which your answer can be read. It may take some practice at first: A lack of readable shapes in the wax is usually the result of an impatient pouring technique or improper concentration. After a few tries, though, the congealed wax will present an infinite variety of shapes. Below are some traditional interpretations of common wax shapes.

If the reader sees an elephant, it is likely that the querent will marry money or receive an inheritance from a male relative. A spider indicates the meddling of others in your affairs and should be interpreted as unfortunate. If there appears the shape of an altar, there will be consolation for your troubles. A column signifies financial gains, or a large and lasting fortune. A single cross assures you of a peaceful death, while three crosses predict employment in high positions. A wheel predicts change, though it does not specify whether the change will be for the better or worse.

A horse is a sign of runaway passion and recklessness. A dagger warns of jealousy and vengeance. Peacocks caution the querent against excessive pride. A rabbit speaks of fertility, just as human figures foretell an increase in members of the family circle. Imperfect or badly formed human figures, however, speak of a scandal or personal exposé.

The sun indicates rising powers, the moon a period of rest and contemplation. Serpents warn of temptation or falling victim to the wiles of others. Insects and fish warn of danger. Birds always tell of the desire for freedom. Houses foretell material gain. Ships tell of travel, while walls speak of solid achievements.

Mountains or hills mean strength and good luck. Clouds or smoke indicate something unseen or currently unknowable. Simple spill formations speak of an end to your troubles, as do broken branches or swords.

Always remember to read all the shapes that may appear together. For instance, a bird flying over a mountain may indicate a querent's desire to be freed from a role of strength; perhaps he or she feels they have too much responsibility or that someone depends upon them too much.

For further symbolic references, see the sections on coffee-ground- and tealeaf-reading, and, of course, always rely on your intuition and knowledge of human nature in readings of this kind. Some may find divination by wax preferable to its cousins, however, simply because, unlike coffee-ground- or tealeaf-reading, it does not require a fine eye, and the shapes themselves solidify, making it possible to refer to them over a period of time. Divination by wax can very well be a bolder and clearer process for the novice than cup-reading, simply because the shapes are easier to read and less disputable.

Wells

Wells have a great deal of sacred significance. Originally the site of many pagan oracles and temples, probably because of the curative powers of water and the mysterious nature of sunken wells themselves, people have returned to them time and again to query the future. With the advent of Christianity, many pagan wells were given saints' names, and well divination took on an oddly Christian tenor. At Sainte-Eugenia, in Brittany, vindictive people threw pins in the well in an attempt to do harm to their enemies.

A famous well in Wales foretold death. Cocks or hens were carried around the well and then taken to a graveyard. The sick person, meanwhile, was hauled to church, where he or she spent the night with a Bible under his or her head. If the hen or cock died, the person would get well. It was recommended that a coin offering be left upon the altar.

Well water was often drunk with ceremony on holy days in order to effect cures and ward off danger or evil. In most cases, whether a person went for consultation or for healing, it was the custom to toss pins, needles, buttons, or coins into the well as an afterthought—probably the tradition from which our current wishing-well and fountain lore stems.

Writing, Automatic

Automatic writing is one of the few forms of divination that involves a kind of channeling or mediumship. The writer is, in effect, temporarily taken over by the spiritual presence of another, who then writes any messages, using the body of the subject. The main distinction is that the diviner or writer does not interpret the writing or communications until after the writing has been completed and the session is over. Not everyone is suited to this form of communication, but for those who want to give it a try, we include the following method.

Sit comfortably in a chair at a table and clear your mind of any thoughts and distractions. Mentally bathe yourself in the white light of protection. Using an oversized sketch pad, take up a pencil and allow your mind to float. Your hand and arm will begin to move in large random patterns. An increase in speed or a change in the shapes drawn is usually indicative that a spirit is present. It is best to have one or more people present, one of whom should sit close to you and turn the pages as the pages of the pad are filled. Others may then begin their inquiry, either by asking specific questions or by reading the messages and prompting further communication as needed. Again, be sure to try this method with those you trust and on whom you can depend. If it appears that the spiritual presence is not of the Light or is somehow disturbing, simply instruct one of the people present to softly call your name. When the writing is finished, you will come back to yourself naturally in a few moments and can study the writing, further illuminating it with any personal impression of the visitation.

Bibliography

Baynes, C. F., and R. Wilhelm, editors. *The I Ching.* Princeton University Press, 1968.

Blum, Ralph. *The Book of Runes.* St. Martin's Press, 1982.

Campell, John Gregorson. *Witchcraft and Second Sight in the Highlands and Island of Scotland.* Singing Tree Press, 1970.

Cavendish, Richard, editor. *Man, Myth and Magic* (seven volumes). Purnell, 1972.

Christian, Paul. *History and Practice of Magic.* Citadel Press, 1969.

Cunningham, Scott. *Magical Herbalism.* Llewellyn, 1985.

Daniels, Elizabeth. *Fortune in Your Hand.* Squire, New American Library, 1968.

Dorson, Richard M. *Buying the Wind: Regional Folklore in the United States.* University of Chicago Press, 1964.

Fagan, Brian M. *The Aztecs.* W. H. Freeman, 1984.

Fitzherbert, Andrew. *Hand Psychology.* Angus & Robertson, 1986.

Gray, Eden. *Mastering the Tarot.* New American Library, 1973.

———. *The Tarot Revealed.* New American Library, 1969.

Hole, Christina. *Witchcraft in England.* Batsford, 1947.

Kaplan, Stewart R. *Encyclopedia of Tarot.* U.S. Games System, 1978.

King, Francis X. *The Encyclopedia of Fortune Telling.* Gallery Books, 1988.

Sullivan, Kevin. *The Crystal Handbook.* New American Library, 1987.

Van Orr, Raymond, editor. *I Ching.* New American Library, 1971.

Waite, A. E. *Pictorial Guide to the Tarot.* Rider, 1910.

Wing, R. L. *The Illustrated I Ching.* Dolphin-Doubleday, 1982.

Signet Supernatural

Buy them at your local

bookstore or use coupon

on next page for ordering.

27 million Americans can't read a bedtime story to a child.

It's because 27 million adults in this country simply can't read.

Functional illiteracy has reached one out of five Americans. It robs them of even the simplest of human pleasures, like reading a fairy tale to a child.

You can change all this by joining the fight against illiteracy.

Call the Coalition for Literacy at toll-free **1-800-228-8813** and volunteer.

Volunteer Against Illiteracy. The only degree you need is a degree of caring.